VINTAGE **MURAKAMI**

Haruki Murakami was born in Kyoto, Japan, in 1949. He grew up in Kobe and graduated from Waseda University in Tokyo. His first novel, *Hear the Wind Sing* (1979), won him the Gunzou Literature Prize for budding writers. This novel, together with *Pinball 1973* (1980) and *A Wild Sheep Chase* (1982), for which he won the Noma Literary Prize for New Writers, form The Trilogy of the Rat. He is also the author of *Hard-Boiled Wonderland and the End of the World* (1985), *Norwegian Wood* (1987), *Dance Dance Dance* (1988), *South of the Border, West of the Sun* (1992), and *The Elephant Vanishes* (1993). In 1991, Murakami spent four years in the United States with his wife where he taught at Princeton and wrote *The Wind-Up Bird Chronicle* (1994). After the Kobe earthquake and the poison gas attack in the Tokyo subway in 1995, Murakami returned to Japan where he interviewed attack victims, and then members of the religious cult Aum Shinrikyo. From these interviews, Murakami published two nonfiction books in Japan, the later of which, *The Place That Was Promised* (1998), won the Kuwabara Takeo Academic Award. These two books were selectively combined to form the English edition *Underground* (2000). Since then, Murakami has written *Sputnik Sweetheart* (1999) and *after the quake* (2002). The most recent of his many honors is the Yomiuri Literary Prize, whose previous recipients include Yukio Mishima, Kenzaburo Oe, and Kobo Abe. His work has been translated into thirty-four languages.

BOOKS BY HARUKI MURAKAMI

A Wild Sheep Chase

Hard-Boiled Wonderland and the End of the World

Norwegian Wood

The Elephant Vanishes

Dance Dance Dance

The Wind-Up Bird Chronicle

South of the Border, West of the Sun

Sputnik Sweetheart

Underground

after the quake

VINTAGE MURAKAMI

Haruki Murakami

VINTAGE BOOKS

A Division of Random House, Inc.

New York

A VINTAGE ORIGINAL, JANUARY 2004

Published in the United States by Vintage Books, a division of Random House, Inc., New York, and simultaneously in Canada by Random House of Canada Limited, Toronto.

Library of Congress Cataloging-in-Publication Data
Murakami, Haruki, 1949–.
Vintage Murakami / Haruki Murakami.
p. cm.
ISBN 1-4000-3396-9
Contents: "Barn burning" from The Elephant vanishes—"Shizuko Akashi" from Underground—"honey pie" from after the quake—"Lieutenant Mamiya's long story: Part I" from The Wind-up bird chronicle—"Lieutenant Mamiya's long story: Part II" from The Wind-up bird chronicle—"Ice man."
I. Title.
PL856.U673 A2 2004
895.6'35—dc21 2003049700

Book design by JoAnne Metsch

www.vintagebooks.com

Printed in the United States of America
10 9 8 7 6 5 4 3 2 1

CONTENTS

VINTAGE MURAKAMI

Chapter One

from NORWEGIAN WOOD

I was thirty-seven then, strapped in my seat as the huge 747 plunged through dense cloud cover on approach to the Hamburg airport. Cold November rains drenched the earth and lent everything the gloomy air of a Flemish landscape: the ground crew in rain gear, a flag atop a squat airport building, a BMW billboard. So—Germany again.

Once the plane was on the ground, soft music began to flow from the ceiling speakers: a sweet orchestral cover version of the Beatles' "Norwegian Wood." The melody never failed to send a shudder through me, but this time it hit me harder than ever.

I bent forward in my seat, face in hands to keep my skull from splitting open. Before long one of the German stewardesses approached and asked in English if I were sick. "No," I said, "just dizzy."

"Are you sure?"

"Yes, I'm sure. Thanks."

She smiled and left, and the music changed to a Billy Joel tune. I straightened up and looked out the plane window at the dark clouds hanging over the North Sea, thinking of what I had lost in the course of my life: times gone forever, friends who had died or disappeared, feelings I would never know again.

The plane reached the gate. People began unlatching their seatbelts and pulling baggage from the storage bins, and all the while I was in the meadow. I could smell the grass, feel the wind on my face, hear the cries of the birds. Autumn 1969, and soon I would be twenty.

The stewardess came to check on me again. This time she sat next to me and asked if I was all right.

"I'm fine, thanks," I said with a smile. "Just feeling kind of blue."

"I know what you mean," she said. "It happens to me, too, every once in a while."

She stood and gave me a lovely smile. "Well, then, have a nice trip. *Auf Wiedersehen.*"

"Auf Wiedersehen."

EIGHTEEN years have gone by, and still I can bring back every detail of that day in the meadow. Washed clean of summer's dust by days of gentle rain, the mountains wore a deep, brilliant green. The October breeze set white fronds of head-tall grasses swaying. One long streak of cloud hung pasted across a dome of frozen blue. It almost hurt to look at that far-off sky. A puff of wind swept across the meadow and through her hair before it slipped into the woods to rustle branches and send back snatches of distant barking—a hazy sound that seemed to reach us from the doorway to another world. We heard no other sounds. We met no other people. We saw only two bright, red birds leap startled from the center of the meadow and dart into the woods. As we ambled along, Naoko spoke to me of wells.

Memory is a funny thing. When I was in the scene, I hardly paid it any mind. I never stopped to think of it as something that would make a lasting impression, certainly never imagined that eighteen years later I would recall it in such detail. I didn't give a damn about the scenery that day. I was thinking about myself. I was thinking about the beautiful girl walking next to me. I was thinking about the two of us together, and then about myself again. It was the age, that time of life when every sight, every feeling, every thought came back, like a boomerang, to me. And worse, I was in love. Love with complications. Scenery was the last thing on my mind.

Now, though, that meadow scene is the first thing that comes back to me. The smell of the grass, the faint chill of the wind, the line of the hills, the barking of a dog: these are the first things, and they come with absolute clarity. I feel as if I can reach out and trace them with a fingertip. And yet, as clear as the scene may be, no one is in it. No one. Naoko is not there, and neither am I. Where could we have disappeared to? How could such a thing have happened? Everything that seemed so important back then—Naoko, and the self I was then, and the world I had then: where could they have all gone? It's true, I can't even bring back Naoko's face—not right away, at least. All I'm left holding is a background, sheer scenery, with no people up front.

True, given time enough, I can bring back her face. I start joining images—her tiny, cold hand; her straight, black hair so smooth and cool to the touch; a soft, rounded earlobe and the microscopic mole just beneath it; the camel's hair coat she wore in the winter; her habit of looking straight into your eyes when asking a question; the slight trembling that would come to her voice now and then (as if she were speaking on a windy hilltop)—and suddenly her face is there, always in profile at first, because Naoko and I were always out walking together, side by side. Then she turns to me, and smiles, and tilts her head just a bit, and begins to speak, and she looks into my eyes as if trying to catch the image of a minnow that has darted across the pool of a limpid spring.

I do need that time, though, for Naoko's face to appear. And as the years have passed, the time has grown longer. The sad truth is that what I could recall in five seconds all too soon needed ten, then thirty, then a full minute—like shadows lengthening at dusk. Someday, I suppose, the shadows will be swallowed up in darkness. There is no way around it: my memory is growing ever more distant from the spot where Naoko used to stand—ever more distant from the spot where my old self used to stand. And nothing but scenery, that view of the meadow in October, returns again and again to me like a symbolic scene in a movie. Each time it appears, it delivers a kick to some part of my mind. "Wake up," it says. "I'm still here. Wake up and think about it. Think about why I'm still here." The kicking never hurts me. There's no pain at all. Just a hollow sound that echoes with each kick. And even that is bound to fade one day. At the Hamburg airport, though, the kicks were longer and harder than usual. Which is why I am writing this book. To think. To understand. It just happens to be the way I'm made. I have to write things down to feel I fully comprehend them.

LET'S see, now, what was Naoko talking about that day?

Of course: the "field well." I have no idea whether such a well ever existed. It might have been an image or a sign that existed only inside Naoko, like all the other things she used to spin into existence inside her mind in those dark days. Once she had described it to me, though,

I was never able to think of that meadow scene without the well. From that day forward, the image of a thing I had never laid eyes on became inseparably fused to the actual scene of the field that lay before me. I can go so far as to describe the well in minute detail. It lay precisely on the border where the meadow ended and the woods began—a dark opening in the earth a yard across, hidden by the meadow grass. Nothing marked its perimeter—no fence, no stone curb (at least not one that rose above ground level). It was nothing but a hole, a mouth open wide. The stones of its collar had been weathered and turned a strange muddy white. They were cracked and had chunks missing, and a little green lizard slithered into an open seam. You could lean over the edge and peer down to see nothing. All I knew about the well was its frightening depth. It was deep beyond measuring, and crammed full of darkness, as if all the world's darknesses had been boiled down to their ultimate density.

"It's really, *really* deep," said Naoko, choosing her words with care. She would speak that way sometimes, slowing down to find the exact word she was looking for. "But no one knows where it is," she continued. "The one thing I know for sure is that it's around here somewhere."

Hands thrust into the pockets of her tweed jacket, she smiled at me as if to say "It's true!"

"Then it must be incredibly dangerous," I said. "A

deep well, but nobody knows where it is. You could fall in and that'd be the end of you."

"The end. Aaaaaaah, splat. Finished."

"Things like that must actually happen."

"They do, every once in a while. Maybe once in two or three years. Somebody disappears all of a sudden, and they just can't find him. So then the people around here say, 'Oh, he fell in the field well.'"

"Not a nice way to die," I said.

"No, it's a terrible way to die," said Naoko, brushing a cluster of grass seed from her jacket. "The best thing would be to break your neck, but you'd probably just break your leg and then you couldn't do a thing. You'd yell at the top of your lungs, but nobody'd hear you, and you couldn't expect anybody to find you, and you'd have centipedes and spiders crawling all over you, and the bones of the ones who died before are scattered all around you, and it's dark and soggy, and way overhead there's this tiny, tiny circle of light like a winter moon. You die there in this place, little by little, all by yourself."

"Yuck, just thinking about it makes my flesh creep," I said. "Somebody should find the thing and build a wall around it."

"But nobody *can* find it. So make sure you don't go off the path."

"Don't worry, I won't."

Naoko took her left hand from her pocket and squeezed my hand. "Don't *you* worry," she said. "You'll be OK. *You* could go running all around here in the middle of the night and you'd *never* fall into the well. And as long as I stick with you, I won't fall in, either."

"Never?"

"Never!"

"How can you be so sure?"

"I just know," she said, increasing her grip on my hand and continuing on for a ways in silence. "I know these things. I'm always right. It's got nothing to do with logic: I just feel it. For example, when I'm really close to you like this, I'm not the least bit scared. Nothing dark or evil could ever tempt me."

"Well, that answers that," I said. "All you have to do is stay with me like this all the time."

"Do you mean that?"

"Of course I mean it."

Naoko stopped short. So did I. She put her hands on my shoulders and peered into my eyes. Deep within her own pupils a heavy, black liquid swirled in a strange whirlpool pattern. Those beautiful eyes of hers were looking inside me for a long, long time. Then she stretched to her full height and touched her cheek to mine. It was a marvelous, warm gesture that stopped my heart for a moment.

"Thank you," she said.

"My pleasure," I answered.

"I'm so happy you said that. Really happy," she said with a sad smile. "But it's impossible."

"Impossible? Why?"

"It would be wrong. It would be terrible. It—"

Naoko clamped her mouth shut and started walking again. I could tell that all kinds of thoughts were whirling around in her head, so rather than intrude on them I kept silent and walked by her side.

"It would just be wrong—wrong for you, wrong for me," she said after a long pause.

"Wrong how?" I murmured.

"Don't you see? It's just not possible for one person to watch over another person for ever and ever. I mean, say we got married. You'd have to go to work during the day. Who's going to watch over me while you're away? Or say you have to go on a business trip, who's going to watch over me then? Can I be glued to you every minute of our lives? What kind of equality would there be in that? What kind of relationship would that be? Sooner or later you'd get sick of me. You'd wonder what you were doing with your life, why you were spending all your time babysitting this woman. I couldn't stand that. It wouldn't solve any of my problems."

"But your problems are not going to continue for the rest of your life," I said, touching her back. "They'll end eventually. And when they do, we'll stop and think about how to go on from there. Maybe *you* will have to help *me.*

We're not running our lives according to some account book. If you need me, use me. Don't you see? Why do you have to be so rigid? Relax, let your guard down. You're all tensed up so you always expect the worst. Relax your body, and the rest of you will lighten up."

"How can you say that?" she asked in a voice drained of feeling.

Naoko's voice alerted me to the possibility that I had said something I shouldn't have.

"Tell me how you could say such a thing," she said, staring down at the ground beneath her feet. "You're not telling me anything I don't know already. 'Relax your body, and the rest of you will lighten up.' What's the point of saying that to me? If I relaxed my body now, I'd fall apart. I've always lived like this, and it's the only way I know how to go on living. If I relaxed for a second, I'd never find my way back. I'd go to pieces, and the pieces would be blown away. Why can't you see that? How can you talk about watching over me if you can't see that?"

I said nothing in return.

"I'm confused. Really confused. And it's a lot deeper than you think. Deeper . . . darker . . . colder. But tell me something. How could you have slept with me that time? How could you have done such a thing? Why didn't you just leave me alone?"

Now we were walking through the frightful silence of a pine wood. The desiccated corpses of cicadas that had died at the end of the summer littered the surface of the path, crunching beneath our shoes. As if searching for something we'd lost, Naoko and I continued slowly down the path in the woods.

"I'm sorry," she said, taking my arm and shaking her head. "I didn't mean to hurt you. Try not to let what I said bother you. Really, I'm sorry. I was just angry at myself."

"I guess I don't really understand you yet," I said. "I'm not all that smart. It takes me a while to understand things. But if I *do* have the time, I *will* come to understand you—better than anyone else in the world ever can."

We came to a stop and stood in the silent woods, listening. I tumbled pinecones and cicada shells with the toe of my shoe, then looked up at the patches of sky showing through the pine branches. Hands thrust in her jacket pockets, Naoko stood there thinking, her eyes focused on nothing in particular.

"Tell me something, Toru," she said. "Do you love me?"

"You know I do," I answered.

"Will you do me two favors?"

"You may have up to three wishes, madame."

Naoko smiled and shook her head. "No, two will be enough. One is for you to realize how grateful I am that you came to see me here. I hope you'll understand how happy you've made me. I know it's going to save me if anything will. I may not show it, but it's true."

"I'll come to see you again," I said. "And what is the other wish?"

"I want you always to remember me. Will you remember that I existed, and that I stood next to you here like this?"

"Always," I said. "I'll always remember."

She walked on ahead without speaking. The autumn light filtering through the branches danced over the shoulders of her jacket. A dog barked again, closer than before. Naoko climbed a small mound of a hill, stepped out of the pine wood, and hurried down a gentle slope. I followed two or three steps behind.

"Come over here," I called toward her back. "The well might be around here somewhere." Naoko stopped and smiled and took my arm. We walked the rest of the way side by side.

"Do you really promise never to forget me?" she asked in a near whisper.

"I'll never forget you," I said. "I *could* never forget you."

EVEN so, my memory has grown increasingly distant, and I have already forgotten any number of things. Writing from memory like this, I often feel a pang of dread. What if I've forgotten the most important thing? What if somewhere inside me there is a dark limbo where all the truly important memories are heaped and slowly turning into mud?

Be that as it may, it's all I have to work with. Clutching these faded, fading, imperfect memories to my breast, I go on writing this book with all the desperate intensity of a starving man sucking on bones. This is the only way I know to keep my promise to Naoko.

Once, long ago, when I was still young, when the memories were far more vivid than they are now, I often tried to write about Naoko. But I was never able to produce a line. I knew that if that first line would come, the rest would pour itself onto the page, but I could never make it happen. Everything was too sharp and clear, so that I could never tell where to start—the way a map that shows too much can sometimes be useless. Now, though, I realize that all I can place in the imperfect vessel of writing are imperfect memories and imperfect thoughts. The more the memories of Naoko inside me fade, the more deeply I am able to understand her. I know, too, why she asked me not to forget her. Naoko herself knew, of course. She knew that my memories of her would fade. Which is precisely why she begged me never to forget her, to remember that she had existed.

The thought fills me with an almost unbearable sorrow. Because Naoko never loved me.

—Translated by Jay Rubin

BARN BURNING

I met her at the wedding party of an acquaintance and we got friendly. This was three years ago. We were nearly a whole generation apart in age—she twenty, myself thirty-one—but that hardly got in the way. I had plenty of other things to worry my head about at the time, and to be perfectly honest, I didn't have a spare moment to think about age difference. And our ages never bothered her from the very beginning. I was married, but that didn't matter, either. She seemed to consider things like age and family and income to be of the same a priori order as shoe size and vocal pitch and the shape of one's fingernails. The sort of thing that thinking about won't change one bit. And that much said, well, she had a point.

She was working as an advertising model to earn a living while studying pantomime under somebody-or-other, a famous teacher, apparently. Though the work end of things was a drag and she was always turning down jobs her agent lined up, so her money situation was really rather precarious. But whatever she lacked in take-home pay she probably made up for on the goodwill of a number of boyfriends. Naturally, I don't know this for certain; it's just what I pieced together from snippets of her conversation.

Still, I'm not suggesting there was even a glimmer of a hint that she was sleeping with guys for money. Though perhaps she did come close to that on occasion. Yet even if she did, that was not an essential issue; the essentials were surely far more simple. And the long and short of it was, this guileless simplicity is what attracted a particular kind of person. The kind of men who had only to set eyes on this simplicity of hers before they'd be dressing it up with whatever feelings they held inside. Not exactly the best explanation, but even she'd have to admit it was this simplicity that supported her.

Of course, this sort of thing couldn't go on forever. (If it could, we'd have to turn the entire workings of the universe upside down.) The possibility did exist, but only under specific circumstances, for a specific period. Just like with "peeling mandarin oranges."

"Peeling mandarin oranges?" you say?

When we first met, she told me she was studying pantomime.

Oh, really, I'd said, not altogether surprised. Young women are all into *something* these days. Plus, she didn't look like your die-cast polish-your-skills-in-dead-earnest type.

Then she "peeled a mandarin orange." Literally, that's what she did: She had a glass bowl of oranges to her left and another bowl for the peels to her right—so went the setup—in fact, there was nothing there. She proceeded to pick up one imaginary orange, then slowly peel it, pop pieces into her mouth, and spit out the pulp one section at a time, finally disposing of the skin-wrapped residue into the right-hand bowl when she'd eaten the entire fruit. She repeated this maneuver again and again. In so many words, it doesn't sound like much, but I swear, just watching her do this for ten or twenty minutes—she and I kept up a running conversation at the counter of this bar, her "peeling mandarin oranges" the whole while, almost without a second thought—I felt the reality of everything around me being siphoned away. Unnerving, to say the least. Back when Eichmann stood trial in Israel, there was talk that the most fitting sentence would be to lock him in a cell and gradually remove all the air. I don't really know how he did meet his end, but that's what came to mind.

"Seems you're quite talented," I said.

"Oh, this is nothing. Talent's not involved. It's not a

question of making yourself believe there *is* an orange there, you have to forget there *isn't* one. That's all."

"Practically Zen."

That's when I took a liking to her.

We generally didn't see all that much of each other. Maybe once a month, twice at the most. I'd ring her up and invite her out somewhere. We'd eat out or go to a bar. We talked intensely; she'd hear me out and I'd listen to whatever she had to say. We hardly had any common topics between us, but so what? We became, well, pals. Of course, I was the one who paid the bill for all the food and drinks. Sometimes she'd call me, typically when she was broke and needed a meal. And then it was unbelievable the amount of food she could put away.

When the two of us were together, I could truly relax. I'd forget all about work I didn't want to do and trivial things that'd never be settled anyway and the crazy mixed-up ideas that crazy mixed-up people had taken into their heads. It was some kind of power she had. Not that there was any great meaning to her words. And if I did catch myself interjecting polite nothings without really tuning in what she was saying, there still was something soothing to my ears about her voice, like watching clouds drift across the far horizon.

I did my share of talking, too. Everything from personal matters to sweeping generalities, I told her my honest thoughts. I guess she also let some of my verbiage go by, likewise with minimum comment. Which was fine by me. It was a mood I was after, not understanding or sympathy.

Then two years ago in the spring, her father died of a heart ailment, and she came into a small sum of money. At least, that's how she described it. With the money, she said, she wanted to travel to North Africa. Why North Africa, I didn't know, but I happened to know someone working at the Algerian embassy, so I introduced her. Thus she decided to go to Algeria. And as things took their course, I ended up seeing her off at the airport. All she carried was a ratty old Boston bag stuffed with a couple of changes of clothes. By the look of her as she went through the baggage check, you'd almost think she was returning from North Africa, not going there.

"You really going to come back to Japan in one piece?" I joked.

"Sure thing. 'I shall return,'" she mocked.

Three months later, she did. Three kilos lighter than when she left and tanned about six shades darker. With her was her new guy, whom she presented as someone she met at a restaurant in Algiers. Japanese in Algeria were all too few, so the two of them easily fell in together and eventually became intimate. As far I know, this guy was her first real regular lover.

He was in his late twenties, tall, with a decent build,

and rather polite in his speech. A little lean on looks, perhaps, though I suppose you could put him in the handsome category. Anyway, he struck me as nice enough; he had big hands and long fingers.

The reason I know so much about the guy is that I went to meet her when she arrived. A sudden telegram from Beirut had given a date and a flight number. Nothing else. Seemed she wanted me to come to the airport. When the plane got in—actually, it was four hours late due to bad weather, during which time I read three magazines cover to cover in a coffee lounge—the two of them came through the gate arm in arm. They looked like a happy young married couple. When she introduced us, he shook my hand, virtually in reflex. The healthy handshake of those who've been living a long time overseas. After that, we went into a restaurant. She was dying to have a bowl of tempura and rice, she said; meanwhile, he and I both had beer.

He told me he worked in trading but didn't offer any more details. I couldn't tell whether he simply didn't want to talk business or was thoughtfully sparing me a boring exposition. Nor, in truth, did I especially want to hear about trading, so I didn't press him. With little else to discuss, the conversation meandered between safety on the streets of Beirut and water supplies in Tunis. He proved to be quite well informed about affairs over the whole of North Africa and the Middle East.

By now she'd finished her tempura and announced with a big yawn that she was feeling sleepy. I half expected her to doze off on the spot. She was precisely the type who could fall asleep anywhere. The guy said he'd see her home by taxi, and I said I'd take the train as it was faster. Just why she had me come all the way out to the airport was beyond me.

"Glad I got to meet you," he told me, as if to acknowledge the inconvenience.

"Same here," I said.

THEREAFTER I met up with the guy a number of times. Whenever I ran into her, he was always by her side. I'd make a date with her, and he'd drive up in a spotless silver-gray German sports car to let her off. I know next to nothing about automobiles, but it reminded me of those jaunty coupes you see in old black-and-white Fellini films. Definitely not the sort of car your ordinary salaryman owns.

"The guy's got to be loaded," I ventured to comment to her once.

"Yeah," she said without much interest, "I guess."

"Can you really make that much in trading?"

"Trading?"

"That's what he said. He works in trading."

"Okay, then, I imagine so. . . But hey, what do I know?

He doesn't seem to do much work at all, as far as I can see. He does his share of seeing people and talking on the phone, I'll say that, though."

The young man and his money remained a mystery.

THEN one Sunday afternoon in October, she rang up. My wife had gone off to see some relatives that morning and left me alone at home. A pleasant day, bright and clear, it found me idly gazing at the camphor tree outside and enjoying the new autumn apples. I must have eaten a good seven of them that day—it was either a pathological craving or some kind of premonition.

"Listen," she said right off, "just happened to be heading in your direction. Would it be all right if we popped over?"

"We?" I threw back the question.

"Me and him," came her self-evident reply.

"Sure," I had to say, "by all means."

"Okay, we'll be there in thirty minutes," she said, then hung up.

I lay there on the sofa awhile longer before taking a shower and shaving. As I toweled myself dry, I wondered whether to tidy up around the house but canned the idea. There wasn't time. And despite the piles of books and magazines and letters and records, the occasional pencil here or sweater there, the place didn't seem particularly dirty. I sat back down on the sofa, looked at the camphor tree, and ate another apple.

They showed up a little past two. I heard a car stop in front of the house, and went to the front door to see her leaning out the window of the silver-gray coupe, waving. I directed them to the parking space around back.

"We're here," she beamed, all smiles. She wore a sheer blouse that showed her nipples, and an olive-green mini-skirt. He sported a navy blazer, but there was something else slightly different about him; maybe it was the two-day growth of beard. Not at all slovenly looking, it even brought out his features a shade. As he stepped from the car, he removed his sunglasses and shoved them into his breast pocket.

"Terribly sorry to be dropping in on you like this on your day off," he apologized.

"Not at all, don't mind a bit. Every day might as well be a day off with me, and I was getting kind of bored here on my own," I allowed.

"We brought some food," she said, lifting a large white paper bag from the backseat of the car.

"Food?"

"Nothing extraordinary," he spoke up. "It's just that, a sudden visit on a Sunday, I thought, why not take along something to eat?"

"Very kind of you. Especially since I haven't had anything but apples all morning."

We went inside and set the groceries out on the table. It turned out to make quite a spread: roast beef sandwiches, salad, smoked salmon, blueberry ice cream—and good quantities at that. While she transferred the food to plates, I grabbed a bottle of white wine from the refrigerator. It was like an impromptu party.

"Well, let's dig in. I'm starved," pronounced her usual ravenous self.

Midway through the feast, having polished off the wine, we tapped into my stock of beer. I can usually hold my own, but this guy could drink; no matter how many beers he downed, his expression never altered in the slightest. Together with her contribution of a couple of cans, we had in the space of a little under an hour racked up a whole tableful of empties. Not bad. Meanwhile, she was pulling records from my shelf and loading the player. The first selection to come on was Miles Davis's "Airegin."

"A Garrard autochanger like that's a rare find these days," he observed. Which launched us into audiophilia, me going on about the various components of my stereo system, him inserting appropriate comments, polite as ever.

The conversation had reached a momentary lull when the guy said, "I've got some grass. Care to smoke?"

I hesitated, for no other reason than I'd only just quit smoking the month before and I wasn't sure what effect it would have. But in the end, I decided to take a toke or two. Whereupon he fished a foil packet from the bottom of the paper bag and rolled a joint. He lit up and took a few puffs to get it started, then passed it to me. It was prime stuff. For the next few minutes we didn't say a word as we each took hits in turn. Miles Davis had finished, and we were now into an album of Strauss waltzes. Curious combination, but what the hell.

After one joint, she was already beat, pleading grass on top of three beers and lack of sleep. I ferried her upstairs and helped her onto the bed. She asked to borrow a T-shirt. No sooner had I handed it to her than she'd stripped to her panties, pulled on the T-shirt, and stretched flat out. By the time I got around to asking if she was going to be warm enough, she had already snoozed off. I went downstairs, shaking my head.

Back in the living room, her guy was busy rolling another joint. Plays hard, this dude. Me, I would have just as soon snuggled into bed next to her and conked right out. Fat chance. We settled down to smoke the second joint, Strauss still waltzing away. Somehow, I was reminded of an elementary-school play. I had the part of the old glove maker. A fox cub comes with money to buy gloves, but the glove maker says it's not enough for a pair.

"'Tain't gonna buy no gloves," I say. Guess I'm something of a villain.

"But Mother's so very c-c-cold. She'll get chapped p-p-paws. P-p-please," says the fox cub.

"Uh-uh, nothing doing. Save your money and come back. Otherwise—"

"Sometimes I burn barns," the guy was saying.

"Excuse me?" I asked. Had I misheard him?

"Sometimes I burn barns," the guy repeated.

I looked at him. His fingertips traced the pattern on his lighter. Then he took a deep draw on the joint and held it in for a good ten seconds before slowly exhaling. The smoke came streaming out of his mouth and into the air like ectoplasm. He passed me the roach.

"Quality product, eh?" he said.

I nodded.

"I brought it from India. Top of the line, the best I could find. Smoke this and, it's strange, I recall all kinds of things. Lights and smells and like that. The quality of memory . . ." He paused and snapped his fingers a few times, as if searching for the right words. ". . . completely changes. Don't you think?"

That it did, I concurred. I really was back in the school play, reexperiencing the commotion on stage, the smell of the paint on the cardboard backdrop.

"I'd like to hear about this barn thing," I said.

He looked at me. His face wore no more expression than ever.

"May I talk about it?" he asked.

"Why not?" I said.

"Pretty simple, really. I pour gasoline and throw a

lighted match. *Flick,* and that's it. Doesn't take fifteen minutes for the whole thing to burn to the ground."

"So tell me," I began, then fell silent. I was having trouble finding the right words, too. "Why is it you burn barns?"

"Is it so strange?"

"Who knows? You burn barns. I don't burn barns. There's this glaring difference, and to me, rather than say which of us is strange, first of all I'd like to clear up just what that difference is. Anyway, it was you who brought up this barn thing to begin with."

"Got me there," he admitted. "You tell it like it is. Say, would you have any Ravi Shankar records?"

No, I didn't, I told him.

The guy spaced out awhile. I could practically see his mind kneading like Silly Putty. Or maybe it was *my* mind that was squirming around.

"I burn maybe one barn every two months," he came back. Then he snapped his fingers again. "Seems to me that's just about the right pace. For me, that is."

I nodded vaguely. Pace?

"Just out of interest, is it your own barns you burn?" I thought to ask.

The guy looked at me uncomprehendingly. "Why have I got to burn my own barns? What makes you think I'd have this surplus of barns, myself?"

"Which means," I continued, "you burn other people's barns, right?"

"Correct," he said. "Obviously. Other people's barns. Which makes it, as it were, a criminal act. Same as you and me smoking this grass here right now. A clear-cut criminal act."

I shut up, elbows on the arms of my chair.

"In other words, I wantonly ignite barns that belong to other people. Naturally, I choose ones that won't cause major fires. All I want to do is simply burn barns."

I nodded and ground out what was left of the roach. "But, if you get caught, you'll be in trouble. Whatever, it's arson, and you might get prison."

"Nobody's going to get caught." He laughed at the very idea. "Pour the gas, light the match, and run. Then I watch the whole thing from a distance through binoculars, nice and easy. Nobody catches me. Really, burn one shitty little barn and the cops hardly even budge."

Come to think of it, they probably wouldn't. On top of which, who'd suspect a well-dressed young man driving a foreign car?

"And does she know about this?" I asked, pointing upstairs.

"Not a thing. Fact is, I've never told anyone else about this but you. I'm not the sort to go spouting off to just anyone."

"So why me?"

The guy extended his fingers of his left hand and stroked his cheek. The growth of beard made a dry, rasping sound. Like a bug walking over a thin, taut sheet of paper. "You're someone who writes novels, so I thought, Wouldn't he be interested in patterns of human behavior and all that? And the way I see it, with novelists, before even passing judgment on something, aren't they the kind who are supposed to appreciate its form? And even if they can't *appreciate* it, they should at least accept it at face value, no? That's why I told you. I wanted to tell you, from my side."

I nodded. Just how was I to accept this at *face value*? From my side, I honestly didn't know.

"This might be a strange way to put it," he took off again, spreading both hands, then bringing them slowly together before his eyes. "But there's a lot of barns in this world, and I've got this feeling that they're all just waiting to be burned. Barns built way off by the seaside, barns built in the middle of rice fields . . . well, anyway, all kinds of barns. But nothing that fifteen minutes wouldn't burn down, nice and neat. It's like that's why they were put there from the very beginning. No grief to anyone. They just . . . vanish. One, two, *poof!*"

"But you're judging that they're not needed."

"I'm not judging anything. They're *waiting* to be burned. I'm simply obliging. You get it? I'm just taking on what's there. Just like the rain. The rain falls. Streams swell. Things get swept along. Does the rain judge anything? Well, all right, does this make me immoral? In my own way, I'd like to believe I've got my own morals. And that's an extremely important force in human existence. A person can't exist without morals. I wouldn't doubt if morals weren't the very balance to my simultaneity."

"Simultaneity?"

"Right, I'm here, and I'm there. I'm in Tokyo, and at the same time I'm in Tunis. I'm the one to blame, and I'm also the one to forgive. Just as a for instance. It's that level of balance. Without such balance, I don't think we could go on living. It's like the linchpin to everything. Lose it and we'd literally go to pieces. But for the very reason that I've got it, simultaneity becomes possible for me."

"So what you're saying is, the act of burning barns is in keeping with these morals of yours?"

"Not exactly. It's an act by which to maintain those morals. But maybe we better just forget the morality. It's not essential. What I want to say is, the world is full of these barns. Me, I got my barns, and you got your barns. It's the truth. I've been almost everywhere in the world. Experienced everything. Came close to dying more than once. Not that I'm proud of it or anything. But okay, let's drop it. My fault for being the quiet type all the time. I talk too much when I do grass."

We fell silent, burned out. I had no idea what to say or

how. I was sitting tight in my mental passenger seat, just watching one weird scene after the next slip past the car window. My body was so loose I couldn't get a good grasp on what the different parts were doing. Yet I was still in touch with the idea of my bodily existence. Simultaneity, if ever there was such a thing: Here I had me thinking, and here I had me observing myself think. Time ticked on in impossibly minute polyrhythms.

"Care for a beer?" I asked a little later.

"Thank you. I would."

I went to the kitchen, brought out four cans and some Camembert, and we helped ourselves.

"When was the last time you burned a barn?" I had to ask.

"Let's see, now." He strained to remember, beer can in hand. "Summer, the end of August."

"And the next time, when'll that be?"

"Don't know. It's not like I work out a schedule or mark dates in my calendar. When I get the urge, I go burn one."

"But, say. When you get this urge, some likely barn doesn't just happen to be lying around, does it?"

"Of course not," he said quietly. "That's why I scout out ones ripe for burning in advance."

"To lay in stock."

"Exactly."

"Can I ask you one more question?"

"Sure."

"Have you already decided on the next barn to burn?"

This caused him to furrow up wrinkles between his eyes; then he inhaled audibly through his nose. "Well, yes. As a matter of fact, I have."

I sipped the last of my beer and said nothing.

"A great barn. The first barn really worth burning in ages. Fact is, I went and checked it out only today."

"Which means, it must be nearby."

"Very near," he confirmed.

So ended our barn talk.

At five o'clock, he roused his girlfriend, and then apologized to me again for the sudden visit. He was completely sober, despite the quantities of beer I'd seen him drink. Then he fetched the sports car from around back.

"I'll keep an eye out for that barn," I told him.

"You do that," he answered. "Like I said, it's right near here."

"What's this about a barn?" she broke in.

"Man talk," he said.

"Oh, great," she fawned.

And at that, the two of them were gone.

I returned to the living room and lay down on the sofa. The table was littered with all manner of debris. I picked up my duffle coat off the floor, pulled it over my head, and conked out.

Bluish gloom and a pungent marijuana odor covered everything. Oddly uneven, that darkness. Lying on the sofa,

I tried to remember what came next in the elementary-school play, but it was long since irretrievable. Did the fox cub ever get the gloves?

I got up from the sofa, opened a window to air the place, went to the kitchen, and made myself some coffee.

THE following day, I went to a bookstore and bought a map of the area where I live. Scaled 20,000:1 and detailed down to the smallest lanes. Then I walked around with the map, penciling in *X*'s wherever there was a barn or shed. For the next three days, I covered four kilometers in all four directions. Living toward the outskirts of town, there are still a good many farmers in the vicinity. So it came to a considerable number of barns—sixteen altogether.

I carefully checked the condition of each of these, and from the sixteen I eliminated all those where there were houses in the immediate proximity or greenhouses alongside. I also eliminated those in which there were farm implements or chemicals or signs that they were still in active use. I didn't imagine he'd want to burn tools or fertilizer.

That left five barns. Five barns worth burning. Or, rather, five barns unobjectionable if burned. The kind of barn it'd take fifteen minutes to reduce to ashes, then no one would miss it. Yet I couldn't decide which would be the one he'd be most likely to torch. The rest was a matter of taste. I was beside myself for wanting to know which of the five barns he'd chosen.

I unfolded my map and erased all but those five *X*'s. I got myself a right angle and a French curve and dividers, and tried to establish the shortest course leaving from my house, going around the five barns, and coming back home again. Which proved to be a laborious operation, what with the roads winding about hills and streams. The result: a course of 7.2 kilometers. I measured it several times, so I couldn't have been too far off.

The following morning at six, I put on my training wear and jogging shoes and ran the course. I run six kilometers every morning anyway, so adding an extra kilometer wouldn't kill me. There were two railroad crossings along the way, but they rarely held you up. And otherwise, the scenery wouldn't be bad.

First thing out of the house, I did a quick circuit around the playing field of the local college, then turned down an unpaved road that ran along a stream for three kilometers. Passing the first barn midway, a path took me through woods. A slight uphill grade, then another barn. A little beyond that were racehorse stables. The Thoroughbreds would be alarmed to see flames—but that'd be it. No real damage.

The third and fourth barns resembled each other like

ugly twins. Set not two hundred meters apart, both were weather-beaten and dirty. You might as well torch the both of them together.

The last barn stood beside a railroad crossing. Roughly the six-kilometer mark. Utterly abandoned, the barn had a tin Pepsi-Cola billboard nailed to the side facing the tracks. The structure—if you could call it that—was such a shambles, I could see it, as he would say, just waiting to be burned.

I paused before this last barn, took a few deep breaths, cut over the crossing, and headed home. Running time: thirty-one minutes thirty seconds. I showered, ate breakfast, stretched out on the sofa to listen to one record, then got down to work.

For one month, I ran the same course each morning. But—no barns burned.

Sometimes, I could swear he was trying to get me to burn a barn. That is, to plant in my head the image of burning barns, so that it would swell up like a bicycle tire pumped with air. I'll grant you, there were times that, well, as long as I was waiting around for him to do the deed, I half considered striking the match myself. It would have been a lot faster. And anyhow, they were only run-down old barns. . . .

Although on second thought, no, let's not get carried away. You won't see me torch any barn. No matter how inflated the image of burning barns grew in my head, I'm really not the type. Me, burn barns? Never. Then what about him? He'd probably just switched prospects. Or else he was too busy and simply hadn't found the time to burn a barn. In any case, there was no word from her.

December came and went, and the morning air pierced the skin. The barns stood their ground, their roofs white with frost. Wintering birds sent the echo of flapping wings through the frozen woods. The world kept in motion unchanged.

THE next time I met the guy was in the middle of December last year. It was Christmas carols everywhere you went. I had gone into town to buy presents for different people, and while walking around Nogizaka I spotted his car. No mistake, his silver-gray sports car. Shinagawa license plate, small dent next to the left headlight. It was parked in the lot of a café, looking less sparkling than when I last saw it, the silver-gray a hint duller. Though maybe that was a mistaken impression on my part: I have this convenient tendency to rework my memories. I dashed into the café without a moment's hesitation.

The place was dark and thick with the strong aroma of coffee. There weren't many voices to be heard, only atmospheric baroque music. I recognized him immediately. He was sitting alone by the window, drinking a café au lait. And though it was warm enough in there to steam up my glasses, he was wearing a black cashmere coat, with his muffler still wrapped around his neck.

I hedged a second, but then figured I might as well approach the guy. I decided not to say I'd seen his car outside; I'd just happened to step in, and by chance there he was.

"Mind if I sit down?" I asked.

"Please, not at all," he replied.

We talked a bit. It wasn't a particularly lively conversation. Clearly, we didn't have much in the way of common topics; moreover, his mind seemed to be on something else. Still, he didn't show any sign of being put out by my presence. At one point, he mentioned a seaport in Tunisia, then he started describing the shrimp they caught there. He wasn't just talking for my sake: He really was serious about these shrimp. All the same, like water to the desert, the story didn't go anywhere before it dissipated.

He signaled to the waiter and ordered a second café au lait.

"Say, by the way, how's your barn doing?" I braved the question.

The trace of a smile came to his lips. "Oh, you still remember?" he said, removing a handkerchief from his pocket to wipe his mouth. "Why, sure, I burned it. Burned it nice and clean. Just as promised."

"One right near my house?"

"Yeah. Really, right by there."

"When?"

"Last—when was it? Maybe ten days after I visited your place."

I told him about how I plotted the barns on my map and ran my daily circuit. "So there's no way I could have *not* seen it," I insisted.

"Very thorough," he gibed, obviously having his fun. "Thorough and logical. All I can say is, you must have missed it. Does happen, you know. Things so close up, they don't even register."

"It just doesn't make sense."

He adjusted his tie, then glanced at his watch. "So very, very close," he underscored. "But if you'll excuse me, I've got to be going. Let's talk about it next time, shall we? Can't keep a person waiting. Sorry."

I had no plausible reason to detain the guy any further.

He stood up, pocketed his cigarettes and lighter, and then remarked, "Oh, by the way, have you seen her lately?"

"No, not at all. Haven't you?"

"Me, neither. I've been trying to get in touch, but she's never in her apartment and she doesn't answer the phone and she hasn't been to her pantomime class the whole while."

"She must have taken off somewhere. She's been known to do that."

The guy stared down at the table, hands buried in his

pockets. "With no money, for a month and a half? As far as making her own way, she hardly has a clue."

He was snapping his fingers in his coat pocket.

"I think I know that girl pretty well, and she absolutely hasn't got yen one. No real friends to speak of. An address book full of names, but that's all they are. She hasn't got anyone she can depend on. No, I take that back, she did trust you. And I'm not saying this out of courtesy. I do believe you're someone special to her. Really, it's enough to make me kind of jealous. And I'm someone who's never ever been jealous at all." He gave a little sigh, then eyed his watch again. "But I really must go. Be seeing you."

Right, I nodded, but no words came. The same as always, whenever I was thrown together with this guy, I became altogether inarticulate.

I tried calling her any number of times after that, but her line had apparently been disconnected. Which somehow bothered me, so I went to her apartment and encountered a locked door, her mailbox stuffed with fliers. The superintendent was nowhere to be found, so I had no way to know if she was even living there anymore. I ripped a page from my appointment book, jotted down "Please contact," wrote my name, and shoved it into the mailbox.

Not a word.

The next time I passed by, the apartment bore the

nameplate of another resident. I actually knocked, but no one was in. And like before, no superintendent in sight.

At that, I gave up. This was one year ago.

She'd disappeared.

EVERY morning, I still run past those five barns. Not one of them has yet burned down. Nor do I hear of any barn fires. Come December, the birds strafe overhead. And I keep getting older.

Although just now and then, in the depths of the night, I'll think about barns burning to the ground.

—*Translated by Alfred Birnbaum*

SHIZUKO AKASHI

Ii-yu-nii-an [Disneyland]

I talked to Shizuko Akashi's elder brother, Tatsuo, on December 2, 1996, and the plan was to visit her at a hospital in a Tokyo suburb the following evening.

I was uncertain whether or not Tatsuo would allow me to visit her until the very last moment. Finally he consented, though only after what must have been a considerable amount of anguished deliberation—not that he ever admitted as much. It's not hard to imagine how indelicate it must have seemed for him to allow a total stranger to see his sister's cruel disability. Or even if it was permissible for me as an individual to see her, the very idea of reporting her condition in a book for all the world to read would surely not go down well with the rest of the family. In this sense, I felt a great responsibility as a writer, not only toward the family but to Shizuko herself.

Yet whatever the consequences, I knew I had to meet Shizuko in order to include her story. Even though I had gotten most of the details from her brother, I felt it only fair that I meet her personally. Then, even if she responded to my questions with complete silence, at least I would have tried to interview her . . .

In all honesty, though, I wasn't at all certain that I would be able to write about her without hurting someone's feelings.

Even as I write, here at my desk the afternoon after seeing her, I lack confidence. I can only write what I saw, praying that no one takes offense. If I can set it all down well enough in words, just maybe . . .

A wintry December. Autumn has slowly slipped past out of sight. I began preparations for this book last December, so that makes one year already. And Shizuko Akashi makes my sixtieth interviewee—though unlike all the others, she can't speak her own mind.

By sheer coincidence, the very day I was to visit Shizuko the police arrested Yasuo Hayashi on faraway Ishigaki Island. The last of the perpetrators to be caught, Hayashi, the so-called Murder Machine, had released three packets of sarin at Akihabara Station on the Hibiya Line, claiming the lives of 8 people and injuring 250. I read the news in the early evening paper, then caught the 5:30 train for

Shizuko's hospital. A police officer had been quoted as saying: "Hayashi had tired of living on the run so long."

Of course, Hayashi's capture would do nothing to reverse the damage he'd already done, the lives he had so radically changed. What was lost on March 20, 1995, will never be recovered. Even so, someone had to tie up the loose ends and apprehend him.

I cannot divulge the name or location of Shizuko's hospital. Shizuko and Tatsuo Akashi are pseudonyms, in keeping with the family's wishes. Actually, reporters once tried to force their way into the hospital to see Shizuko. The shock would surely have set back whatever progress she'd made in her therapy program, not to mention throwing the hospital into chaos. Tatsuo was particularly concerned about that.

Shizuko was moved to the Recuperation Therapy floor of the hospital in August 1995. Until then (for the five months after the gas attack) she had been in the Emergency Care Center of another hospital, where the principal mandate was to "maintain the life of the patient"—a far cry from recuperation. The doctor there had declared it "virtually impossible for Shizuko to wheel herself to the stairs." She'd been confined to bed, her mind in a blur. Her eyes refused to open, her muscles barely moved. Once she was removed to Recuperation, however, her progress exceeded all expectations. She now sits in a wheelchair and moves around the ward with a friendly push from the nurses; she can even manage simple conversations. "Miraculous" is the word.

Nevertheless, her memory has almost totally gone. Sadly, she remembers nothing before the attack. The doctor in charge says she's mentally "about grade-school level," but just what that means Tatsuo doesn't honestly know. Nor do I. Is that the overall level of her thought processes? Is it her synapses, the actual "hardware" of her thinking circuitry? Or is it a question of "software," the knowledge and information she has lost? At this point only a few things can be said with any certainty:

(1) Some mental faculties have been lost.

(2) It is as yet unknown whether they will ever be recovered.

She remembers most of what's happened to her since the attack, but not everything. Tatsuo can never predict what she'll remember and what she'll forget.

Her left arm and left leg are almost completely paralyzed, especially the leg. Having parts of the body immobilized entails various problems: last summer she had to have a painful operation to cut the tendon behind her left knee in order to straighten her crooked left leg.

She cannot eat or drink through her mouth. She cannot yet move her tongue or jaws. Ordinarily we never notice how our tongue and jaws perform complicated maneuvers whenever we eat or drink, wholly unconsciously. Only when we lose these functions do we become acutely aware of their importance. That is Shizuko's situation right now.

She can swallow soft foods like yogurt and ice cream. It has taken long months of patient practice to reach this stage. Shizuko likes strawberry yogurt, sour and sweet, but unfortunately most of her nutrition is still squeezed in by tube through her nose. The air valve that was implanted in her throat while she was hooked up to an artificial respirator still remains. It's now covered with a round metal plate—a blank souvenir of her struggle with death.

Her brother slowly pushes Shizuko's wheelchair out into the lounge area. She's petite, with hair cut short at the fringe. She resembles her brother. Her complexion is good, her eyes slightly glazed as if she has only just woken up. If it wasn't for the plastic tube coming from her nose, she probably wouldn't look handicapped.

Neither eye is fully open, but there is a glint to them—deep in the pupils; a gleam that led me beyond her external appearance to see an inner something that was not in pain.

"Hello," I say.

"Hello," says Shizuko, though it sounds more like *ehh-uoh.*

I introduce myself briefly, with some help from her brother. Shizuko nods. She has been told in advance I was coming.

"Ask her anything you want," says Tatsuo.

I'm at a loss. What on earth can I say?

"Who cuts your hair for you?" is my first question.

"Nurse," comes the answer, or more accurately, *uh-errff*, though in context the word is easy enough to guess. She responds quickly, without hesitation. Her mind is there, turning over at high speed in her head, only her tongue and jaws can't keep pace.

For a while at first Shizuko is nervous, a little shy in front of me. Not that I could tell, but to Tatsuo the difference is obvious.

"What's with you today? Why so shy?" he kids her, but really, when I think about it, what young woman wouldn't be shy about meeting someone for the first time and not looking her healthy best? And if the truth be known, I'm a little nervous myself.

Prior to the interview, Tatsuo had talked to Shizuko about me. "Mr. Murakami, the novelist, says he wants to write about you, Shizuko, in a book. What do you think about that? Is it all right with you? Is it okay if your brother tells him about you? Can he come here to meet you?"

Shizuko answered straightaway, "Yes."

Talking with her, the first thing I notice is her decisive "Yes" and "No," the speed with which she judges things. She readily made up her mind about most things, hardly ever hesitating.

I brought her yellow flowers in a small yellow vase. A color full of life. Sadly, however, Shizuko can't see them. She can make things out only in very bright sunlight. She made a small motion with her head and said, "*Uann-eyhh* [Can't tell]." I just hope that some of the warmth they brought to the room—to my eyes, at least—rubs off atmospherically on her.

She wore a pink cotton gown buttoned to the neck, a light throw over her lap from under which a stiff right hand protruded. Tatsuo, by her side, took up that hand from time to time and patted it lovingly. The hand is always there when words fail.

"Up to now, Shizuko, you've spoken in short words only," says her brother with a smile, "so from our point of view, it's been easier to understand. Recently, though, you seem to want to speak in longer sentences, so it's a bit harder for us to follow. I suppose that means you're making progress, but your mouth still can't keep up."

I can scarcely make out half of what she says. Tatsuo, of course, can discern lots more. The nurses even more still. "The nurses here are all young and earnest and sincere. We owe them a show of gratitude," says Tatsuo. "They're nice people, isn't that right?"

"*Aayiih-ee-uh* [Nice people]," agrees Shizuko.

"But sometimes," Tatsuo continues, "when I don't understand what Shizuko's saying, she gets really angry.

You don't want me to leave before I get what you're saying, do you? Like the last time. Isn't that right, Shizuko?"

Silence. Embarrassed silence.

"Hey, what are you so shy about?" Tatsuo teases her. "You said so yourself, didn't you? You wouldn't let Brother go before he understood."

At that Shizuko finally breaks into a smile. And when she smiles she really lights up. She smiles a lot more than most people, though perhaps she simply has less control over her facial muscles. I'd like to imagine that Shizuko always smiled that way, it blends in so naturally with her face. It strikes me that she and her brother probably carried on this way as children.

"Not long ago," says Tatsuo, "Shizuko would cry and complain—'No, don't go!'—when it was time for me to leave. Each time I repeated the same thing until she gradually stopped fussing: 'Brother has to go home or else the kids will be lonely from waiting. It's not just you, you know, ——— and ——— get lonely too.' Eventually Shizuko got what I was saying, which is great progress, isn't it? Though it must get awfully lonely being left here, I admit."

Silence.

"Which is why I'd like to visit the hospital more often and spend longer talking to my sister," says Tatsuo. In actual fact, however, it's hard enough for Tatsuo to visit the hospital every other day. He has to travel fifty minutes each way back and forth from work.

After work Tatsuo sits with his sister for an hour and talks. He holds her hand, spoon-feeds her strawberry yogurt, coaches her in conversation, fills up the blank spaces in her memory little by little: "We all went there and this is what we did . . ."

"When the memories we share as a family get cut off and lost like this," he says, "that's the hardest thing to accept. It's as if it has been cut away with a knife. . . . Sometimes when I'm going back over the past with her, my voice starts to quaver, then Shizuko asks me, 'Brother, you okay?' "

Hospital visiting hours officially end at eight P.M., but they're less strict with Tatsuo. After the visit, he collects Shizuko's laundry, drives the car back to the office, walks five minutes to the subway, and travels another hour, changing three times before he gets back home. By the time he gets there the kids are asleep. He's kept up this regimen for a year and eight months now. He'd be lying if he said he wasn't exhausted; and no one can honestly say how much longer he'll have to continue.

Hands on the steering wheel on the way back, Tatsuo says: "If this had been caused by an accident or something, I could just about accept it. There'd have been a cause or some kind of reason. But with this totally senseless, idiotic criminal act . . . I'm at my wits' end. I can't take it!" He barely shakes his head, silencing any further comment from me.

"Can you move your right hand a little for me?" I ask Shizuko. And she lifts the fingers of her right hand. I'm sure she's trying, but the fingers move very slowly, patiently grasping, patiently extending. "If you don't mind, would you try holding my hand?"

"*O-eh* [Okay]," she says.

I place four fingers in the palm of her tiny hand—practically the hand of a child in size—and her fingers slowly enfold them, as gently as the petals of a flower going to sleep. Soft, cushioning, girlish fingers, yet far stronger than I had anticipated. Soon they clamp tight over my hand in the way that a child sent on an errand grips that "important item" she's not supposed to lose. There's a strong will at work here, clearly seeking some objective. Focused, but very likely not on me; she's after some "other" beyond me. Yet that "other" goes on a long journey and seems to find its way back to me. Please excuse this nebulous explanation, it's merely a fleeting impression.

Something in her must be trying to break out. I can feel it. A precious something. But it just can't find an outlet. If only temporarily, she's lost the power and means to enable it to come to the surface. And yet that *something* exists unharmed and intact within the walls of her inner space. When she holds someone's hand, it's all she can do to communicate that "this thing is here."

She keeps holding my hand for a very long time, until I say, "Thank you," and slowly, little by little, her fingers unfold.

"Shizuko never says 'hurt' or 'tired,'" Tatsuo tells me driving back later. "She does therapy every day: arm-and-leg training, speech-training, various other programs with specialists—none of it easy, it's tough going—but when the doctor or nurses ask her if she's tired, only three times has she ever said 'Yes.' Three times.

"That's why—as everyone involved agrees—Shizuko has recovered as much as she has. From being unconscious on an artificial respirator to actually talking, it's like something out of a dream."

"What do you want to do when you get well?" I think to ask her.

"Aeh-ehh," she says. I don't understand.

"'Travel,' maybe?" suggests Tatsuo after a moment's thought.

"*Ehf* [Yes]," concurs Shizuko with a nod.

"And where do you want to go?" I ask.

"Ii-yu-nii-an." This no one understands, but with a bit of trial and error it becomes clear she means "Disneyland."

"Ehf," says Shizuko with an emphatic nod.

It's not easy to associate "travel" with "Disneyland." Anyone who lives in Tokyo would not generally consider an outing to Tokyo Disneyland "travel." But in her mind, lacking an awareness of distance, going to Disneyland must be like some great adventure. It's no different, conceptually, than if we were to set out, say, for Greenland. For a fact, going to Disneyland would be a more difficult undertaking for her in practice than for us to travel to the ends of the earth.

Tatsuo's two children—eight and four—remember going to Tokyo Disneyland with their auntie and tell her about it each time they visit the hospital: "It was really fun," they say. So Disneyland as a place has become fixed in her mind as something like a symbol of freedom and health. Nobody knows if Shizuko can actually remember having been there herself. It may only be a later implanted memory. After all, she doesn't even remember her own room where she lived for so long.

Real or imaginary, however, Disneyland is a distinct place in her mind. We can get close to that image, but we can't see the view she sees.

"You want to go to Disneyland with the whole family?" I ask her.

"Ehf," says Shizuko perkily.

"With your brother and sister-in-law and the kids?"

She nods.

Tatsuo looks at me and says, "When she can eat and drink normally with her mouth instead of that tube through her nose, then maybe we can all drive together to Disneyland again." He gives Shizuko's hand a little squeeze.

"I hope that's very very soon," I tell Shizuko.

Shizuko gives another nod. Her eyes are turned in my direction, but she's seeing "something else" beyond me.

"Well, when you get to Disneyland, what ride will you go on?" Tatsuo prompts.

" 'Roller coaster'?" I interpret.

"Space Mountain!" Tatsuo chimes in. "Yeah, you always did like that one."

That evening when I visited the hospital, I'd wanted somehow to encourage her—but how? I'd thought it was up to me, but it wasn't that way at all; no need even to think about giving her encouragement. In the end, it was she who gave *me* encouragement.

In the course of writing this book, I've given a lot of serious thought to the Big Question: what does it mean to be alive? If I were in Shizuko's place, would I have the willpower to live as fully as she? Would I have the courage, or the persistence and determination? Could I hold someone's hand with such warmth and strength? Would the love of others save me? I don't know. To be honest, I'm not so sure.

People the world over turn to religion for salvation. But when religion hurts and maims, where are they to go for salvation? As I talked to Shizuko I tried to look into her eyes now and then. Just what did she see? What lit up those eyes? If ever she gets well enough to speak unhindered, that's something I'd want to ask: "That day I came to visit, what did you see?"

But that day is still far off. Before that comes Disneyland.

—*Translated by Alfred Birnbaum and Philip Gabriel*

HONEY PIE

1

"So Masakichi got his paws full of honey—way more honey than he could eat by himself—and he put it in a bucket, and do-o-o-wn the mountain he went, all the way to the town to sell his honey. Masakichi was the all-time Number One honey bear."

"Do bears have buckets?" Sala asked.

"Masakichi just happened to have one," Junpei explained. "He found it lying in the road, and he figured it would come in handy sometime."

"And it did."

"It really did. So Masakichi the Bear went to town and found a spot for himself in the square. He put up a sign: *Deeelicious Honey. All Natural. One Cup ¥200.*"

"Can bears write?"

"No, of course not," Junpei said. "There was a nice old man with a pencil sitting next to him, and he asked *him* to write it."

"Can bears count money?"

"Absolutely. Masakichi lived with people when he was just a cub, and they taught him how to talk and count money and stuff. Anyway, he was a very talented bear."

"Oh, so he was a little different from ordinary bears."

"Well, yes, just a little. Masakichi was a kind of special bear. And so the other bears, who weren't so special, tended to shun him."

"Shun him?"

"Yeah, they'd go like, 'Hey, what's with this guy, acting so special?' and keep away from him. Especially Tonkichi the tough guy. He really hated Masakichi."

"Poor Masakichi!"

"Yeah, really. Meanwhile, Masakichi *looked* just like a bear, and so the people would say, 'OK, he knows how to count, and he can talk and all, but when you get right down to it he's still a bear.' So Masakichi didn't really belong to either world—the bear world or the people world."

"Poor, poor Masakichi! Didn't he have any friends?"

"Not one. Bears don't go to school, you know, so there's no place for them to make friends."

"*I* have friends," Sala said. "In preschool."

"Of course you do," Junpei said.

"Do *you* have friends, Jun?" "Uncle Junpei" was too long for her, so Sala just called him "Jun."

"Your daddy is my absolute bestest friend from a long, long time ago. And so's your mommy."

"It's good to have friends."

"It *is* good," Junpei said. "You're right about that."

Junpei often made up stories for Sala when she went to bed. And whenever she didn't understand something, she would ask him to explain. Junpei gave a lot of thought to his answers. Sala's questions were always sharp and interesting, and while he was thinking about them he could also come up with new twists to the story.

Sayoko brought a glass of warm milk.

"Junpei is telling me the story of Masakichi the bear," Sala said. "He's the all-time Number One honey bear, but he doesn't have any friends."

"Oh really? Is he a big bear?" Sayoko asked.

Sala gave Junpei an uneasy look. "Is Masakichi big?"

"Not so big," he said. "In fact, he's kind of on the small side. For a bear. He's just about *your* size, Sala. And he's a very sweet-tempered little guy. When he listens to music, he doesn't listen to rock or punk or that kind of stuff. He likes to listen to Schubert all by himself."

Sayoko hummed a little "Trout."

"He listens to music?" Sala asked. "Does he have a CD player or something?"

"He found a boom box lying on the ground one day. He picked it up and brought it home."

"How come all this stuff just happens to be lying around in the mountains?" Sala asked with a note of suspicion.

"Well, it's a very, very steep mountain, and the hikers get all faint and dizzy, and they throw away tons of stuff they don't need. Right there by the road, like, 'Oh man, this pack is so heavy, I feel like I'm gonna die! I don't need this bucket anymore. I don't need this boom box anymore.' Like that. So Masakichi finds everything he needs lying in the road."

"Mommy knows just how they feel," Sayoko said. "Sometimes you want to throw everything away."

"Not *me*," Sala said.

"That's 'cause you're such a greedy little thing," Sayoko said.

"I am *not* greedy," Sala protested.

"No," Junpei said, finding a gentler way to put it: "You're just young and full of energy, Sala. Now hurry and drink your milk so I can tell you the rest of the story."

"OK," she said, wrapping her little hands around the glass and drinking the warm milk with great care. Then she asked, "How come Masakichi doesn't make honey pies and sell them? I think the people in the town would like that better than just plain honey."

"An excellent point," Sayoko said with a smile. "Think of the profit margin!"

"Ah, yes, creating new markets through value added," Junpei said. "This girl will be a real entrepreneur someday."

IT was almost two A.M. by the time Sala went back to bed. Junpei and Sayoko checked to make sure she was asleep, then shared a can of beer at the kitchen table. Sayoko wasn't much of a drinker, and Junpei had to drive home.

"Sorry for dragging you out in the middle of the night," she said, "but I didn't know what else to do. I'm totally exhausted, and you're the only one who can calm her down. There was no way I was going to call Takatsuki."

Junpei nodded, took a slug of beer, and ate one of the crackers on the plate between them.

"Don't worry about me," he said. "I'm awake till the sun comes up, and the roads are empty this time of night. It's no big deal."

"You were working on a story?"

Junpei nodded.

"How's it going?"

"Like always. I write 'em. They print 'em. Nobody reads 'em."

"*I* read them. *All* of them."

"Thanks. You're a nice person," Junpei said. "But the short story is on the way out. Like the slide rule. Anyhow, let's talk about Sala. Has she done this before?"

Sayoko nodded.

"A lot?"

"Almost every night. Sometime after midnight she gets these hysterical fits and jumps out of bed. She can't stop shaking. And I can't get her to stop crying. I've tried everything."

"Any idea what's wrong?"

Sayoko drank what was left of her beer, and stared at the empty glass.

"I think she saw too many news reports on the earthquake. It was too much for a four-year-old. She wakes up at around the time of the quake. She says a man woke her up, somebody she doesn't know. The Earthquake Man. He tries to put her in a little box—way too little for anyone to fit into. She tells him she doesn't want to get inside, but he starts yanking on her arm—so hard her joints crack—and he tries to stuff her inside. That's when she screams and wakes up."

"The Earthquake Man?"

"He's tall and skinny and old. After she's had the dream, she goes around turning on every light in the house and looks for him: in the closets, in the shoe cabinet in the front hall, under the beds, in all the dresser drawers. I tell her it was just a dream, but she won't listen to me. And she won't go to bed until she's looked everywhere he could possibly hide. That takes at least two hours, by which time I'm wide awake. I'm so sleep-deprived I can hardly stand up, let alone work."

Sayoko almost never spilled out her feelings like this.

"Try not to watch the news," Junpei said. "Don't even turn on the TV. The earthquake's all they're showing these days."

"I almost never watch TV anymore. But it's too late now. The Earthquake Man just keeps coming. I went to the doctor, but all he did was give me some kind of sleeping pill to humor me."

Junpei thought for a while.

"How about we go to the zoo on Sunday? Sala says she wants to see a real bear."

Sayoko narrowed her eyes and looked at him. "Maybe. It just might change her mood. Let's do it—the four of us. It's been ages. You call Takatsuki, OK?"

JUNPEI was thirty-six, born and bred in the city of Nishinomiya, Hyogo Prefecture, a quiet residential area in the Shukugawa district. His father owned a pair of jewelry stores, one in Osaka, one in Kobe. He had a sister six years his junior. After a time at a private high school in Kobe, he entered Waseda University in Tokyo. He had passed the entrance exams in both the business and the literature departments. He chose the literature department without the slightest hesitation and told his parents that he had entered the business department. They would never have paid for him to study literature, and Junpei had no intention of wasting four precious years studying the workings of the economy. All he wanted was to study literature, and then to become a novelist.

At the university, he made two friends, Takatsuki and Sayoko. Takatsuki came from the mountains of Nagano. Tall and broad-shouldered, he had been the captain of his high-school soccer team. It had taken him two years of studying to pass the entrance exam, so he was a year older than Junpei. Practical and decisive, he had the kind of looks that made people take to him right away, and he naturally assumed a leadership role in any group. But he had trouble reading books; he had entered the literature department because its exam was the only one he could pass. "What the hell," he said in his positive way. "I'm going to be a newspaper reporter, so I'll let them teach me how to write."

Junpei did not understand why Takatsuki had any interest in befriending him. Junpei was the kind of person who liked to sit alone in his room reading books or listening to music, and he was terrible at sports. Awkward with strangers, he rarely made friends. Still, for whatever reason, Takatsuki seemed to have decided the first time he saw Junpei in class that he was going to make him a friend. He tapped Junpei on the shoulder and said, "Hey, let's get something to eat." And by the end of the day they had opened their hearts to each other.

Takatsuki had Junpei with him when he adopted the

same approach with Sayoko. He tapped her on the shoulder and said, "Hey, how about the three of us get something to eat?" And so their tight little group was born. Junpei, Takatsuki, and Sayoko did everything together. They shared lecture notes, ate lunch in the campus dining hall, talked about their future over coffee between classes, took part-time jobs at the same place, went to all-night movies and rock concerts and walked all over Tokyo, and drank so much beer they even got sick together. In other words, they behaved like first-year college students the world over.

Sayoko was a real Tokyo girl. She came from the old part of town where the merchant class had lived for centuries, and her father ran a shop selling the exquisite little accessories that went with traditional Japanese dress. The business had been in the family for several generations, and it attracted an exclusive clientele that included several famous Kabuki actors. Sayoko had two elder brothers. The first had been groomed to inherit the shop, and the second worked in architectural design. She had graduated from an exclusive girls' prep school, entering the literature department of Waseda with plans to go on to graduate school in English Literature, and ultimately to an academic career. She read a lot, and she and Junpei were constantly exchanging novels and having intense conversations about them.

Sayoko had beautiful hair and intelligent eyes. She

spoke quietly and with simple honesty, but deep down she had great strength. Her expressive mouth bore eloquent testimony to that. She was always casually dressed, without makeup, but she had a unique sense of humor, and her face would crinkle up mischievously whenever she made some funny remark. Junpei found that look of hers beautiful, and he knew that this was the girl he had been searching for. He had never fallen in love until he met Sayoko. He had attended a boys' high school and had had almost no opportunity to meet girls.

But Junpei could never bring himself to express his feelings to Sayoko. He knew that there would be no going back once the words left his mouth, and that she might take herself off somewhere far beyond his reach. At the very least, the perfectly balanced, comfortable relationship of Junpei, Takatsuki, and Sayoko would undergo a shift. So he told himself to leave things as they were for now and watch and wait.

In the end, Takatsuki was the first to make a move. "I hate to throw this at you all of a sudden," he told Junpei, "but I'm in love with Sayoko. I hope you don't mind."

This was midway through September. Takatsuki explained that he and Sayoko had become involved, almost by accident, while Junpei was home in Kansai for the summer vacation.

Junpei fixed his gaze on Takatsuki. It took him a few moments to understand what had happened, but when he did, it sank into him like a lead weight. He no longer had any choice in the matter. "No," he said, "I don't mind."

"I am *so* glad to hear that!" Takatsuki said with a huge grin. "You were the only one I was worried about. I mean, the three of us had such a great thing going, it was kind of like I beat you out. But anyway, Junpei, this had to happen sometime. You have to understand that. If not now, it was bound to happen sooner or later. The main thing is that I want the three of us to go on being friends. OK?"

For the next few days, Junpei felt as if he were trying to walk in deep sand. He skipped classes and work. He lay on the floor of his one-room apartment eating nothing but scraps from the refrigerator and slugging down whiskey whenever the impulse struck him. He thought seriously about quitting the university and going to some distant town where he knew no one and could spend the rest of his years doing manual labor. That would be the best lifestyle for him, he decided.

THE fifth day after he stopped going to classes, Sayoko came to Junpei's apartment. She was wearing a navy blue sweatshirt and white cotton pants, and her hair was pinned back.

"Where have you been?" she asked. "Everybody's worried that you're dead in your room. Takatsuki asked me to check up on you. I guess he wasn't too keen on seeing the corpse himself. He's not as strong as he looks."

Junpei said he had been feeling sick.

"Yeah," she said, "you've lost weight, I think." She stared at him. "Want me to make you something to eat?"

Junpei shook his head. He didn't feel like eating, he said.

Sayoko opened the refrigerator and looked inside with a grimace. It contained only two cans of beer, a deceased cucumber, and some deodorizer. Sayoko sat down next to him. "I don't know how to put this, Junpei, but are you feeling bad about Takatsuki and me?"

Junpei said that he was not. And it was no lie. He was not feeling bad or angry. If, in fact, he was angry, it was at himself. For Takatsuki and Sayoko to become lovers was the most natural thing in the world. Takatsuki had all the qualifications. He himself had none. It was that simple.

"Go halves on a beer?" Sayoko asked.

"Sure."

She took a can of beer from the refrigerator and divided the contents between two glasses, handing one to Junpei. Then they drank in silence, separately.

"It's kind of embarrassing to put this into words," she said, "but I want to stay friends with you, Junpei. Not just for now, but even after we get older. A lot older. I love Takatsuki, but I need you, too, in a different way. Does that make me selfish?"

Junpei was not sure how to answer that, but he shook his head.

Sayoko said, "To understand something and to put that something into a form you can see with your own eyes are two completely different things. If you could manage to do both equally well, though, living would be a lot simpler."

Junpei stared at her in profile. He had no idea what she was trying to say. Why does my brain always have to work so slowly? he wondered. He looked up, and for a long time his half-focused eyes traced the shape of a stain on the ceiling. What would have happened if he had confessed his love to Sayoko before Takatsuki? To this Junpei could find no answer. All he knew for sure was that such a thing could never have happened. Ever.

He heard the sound of tears falling on the tatami, an oddly magnified sound. For a moment he wondered if he was crying without being aware of it. But then he realized that Sayoko was the one who was crying. She had hung her head between her knees, and now, though she made no sound, her shoulders were trembling.

Almost unconsciously, he reached out and put a hand on her shoulder. Then he drew her gently toward him. She did not resist. He wrapped his arms around her and pressed his lips to hers. She closed her eyes and let her lips come open. Junpei caught the scent of tears, and drew breath from her mouth. He felt the softness of her breasts against him. Inside his head, he felt some kind of huge switching of places. He even heard the sound it made, like the creaking of every joint in the world. But that was all. As if regaining consciousness, Sayoko moved her face back and down, pushing Junpei away.

"No," she said quietly, shaking her head. "We can't do this. It's wrong."

Junpei apologized. Sayoko said nothing. They remained that way, in silence, for a long time. The sound of a radio came in through the open window, riding on a breeze. It was a popular song. Junpei felt sure he would remember it till the day he died. In fact, though, try as he might after that, he was never able to bring back the title or the melody.

"You don't have to apologize," Sayoko said. "It's not your fault."

"I think I'm confused," he said honestly.

She reached out and laid her hand on his. "Come back to school, OK? Tomorrow? I've never had a friend like you before. You give me so much. I hope you realize that."

"So much, but not enough," he said.

"That's not true," she said with a resigned lowering of her head. "That is so not true."

JUNPEI went to his classes the next day, and the tight-knit threesome of Junpei, Takatsuki, and Sayoko continued through graduation. Junpei's short-lived desire to disappear disappeared itself with almost magical ease. When he held her in his arms that day in his apartment and pressed his lips to hers, something inside him settled down where it belonged. At least he no longer felt confused. The decision had been made, even if he had not been the one to make it.

Sayoko would sometimes introduce Junpei to old high-school classmates of hers, and they would double-date. He saw a lot of one of the girls, and it was with her that he had sex for the first time, just before his twentieth birthday. But his heart was always somewhere else. He was respectful, kind, and tender to her, but never really passionate or devoted. The only times Junpei became passionate and devoted were when he was alone, writing stories. His girlfriend eventually went elsewhere in search of true warmth. This pattern repeated itself any number of times.

When he graduated, Junpei's parents discovered he had been majoring in literature, not business, and things turned ugly. His father wanted him to come back to Kansai and take over the family firm, but Junpei had no intention of doing that. He wanted to stay in Tokyo and keep writing fiction. There was no room for compromise on either side, and a violent argument ensued. Words were spoken that should not have been. Junpei never saw his parents again, and he was convinced that it had to be that way. Unlike his sister, who always managed to compromise and get along with their parents, Junpei had done nothing but clash with them from the time he was a child. So, he thought with a bitter smile, he had finally been disowned: the upright Confucian parents renounce the decadent scribbler—it was like something out of the Twenties.

Junpei never applied for regular employment, but took a series of part-time jobs that helped him to scrape by as he continued to write. Whenever he finished a story, he showed it to Sayoko to get her honest opinion, then revised it according to her suggestions. Until she pronounced a piece good, he would rewrite again and again, carefully and patiently. He had no other mentor, and he belonged to no writers' group. The one faint lamp he had to guide him was Sayoko's advice.

When he was twenty-four, a story of his won the new writer's prize from a literary magazine, and it was also nominated for the Akutagawa Prize, the coveted gateway to a successful career in fiction. Over the next five years, he was nominated four times for the Akutagawa Prize, but he never won it. He remained the eternally promising candidate. A typical opinion from a judge on the prize committee would say: "For such a young author, this is writing of very high quality, with remarkable examples of both the creation of scene and psychological analysis. But the author has a tendency to let sentiment take over from time to time, and the work lacks both freshness and novelistic sweep."

Takatsuki would laugh when he read such things. "These guys are off their rockers. What the hell is 'novelistic sweep'? Real people don't use words like that. 'Today's sukiyaki was lacking in beefistic sweep.' Ever hear anybody say anything like that?"

Junpei published two volumes of short stories before he turned thirty: *Horse in the Rain* and *Grapes. Horse in the Rain* sold ten thousand copies, *Grapes* twelve thousand. These were not bad figures for a new writer's short story collections, according to his editor. The reviews were generally favorable, but none gave his work passionate support.

Most of Junpei's stories depicted the course of unrequited young love. Their conclusions were always dark, and somewhat sentimental. Everyone agreed they were well written, but they stood unmistakably apart from the more fashionable literature of the day. Junpei's style was lyrical, the plots rather old-fashioned. Readers of his generation were looking for a more inventive style and grittier storylines. This was the age of video games and rap music, after all. Junpei's editor urged him to try a novel. If he never wrote anything but short stories, he would just keep dealing with the same material over and over again, and his fictional world would waste away. Writing a novel could open up whole new worlds for a writer. As a practical matter, too, novels attracted far more attention than stories. If he intended to have a long career, he should recognize that writing only short stories would be a hard way to make a living.

But Junpei was a born short story writer. He would shut himself in his room, let everything else go to hell, and turn out a first draft in three days of concentrated effort. After four more days of polishing, he would give the manuscript to Sayoko and his editor to read, then do more polishing in response to their remarks. Basically, though, the battle was won or lost in that first week. That was when everything that mattered in the story came together. His personality was suited to this way of working: total concentration of effort over a few short days; total concentration of imagery and language. Junpei felt only exhaustion when he thought about writing a novel. How could he possibly maintain and control that mental concentration for months at a time? That kind of pacing eluded him.

He tried, though. He tried over and over again, ending always in defeat. And so he gave up. Like it or not, he was going to have to make his living as a short story writer. That was his style. No amount of effort was going to change his personality. You couldn't turn a great second baseman into a home-run hitter.

Junpei did not need much money to support his austere bachelor's lifestyle. Once he had made what he needed for a given period, he would stop accepting work. He had only one silent cat to feed. The girlfriends he found were always the undemanding type, but even so, they would eventually get on his nerves, and he would come up with some excuse for ending the relationship. Sometimes, maybe once a month, he would wake at an odd time in the night with a feeling close to panic. I'm never going anywhere, he would tell himself. I can struggle all I want, but I'm never going anywhere. Then, he would either force himself to go to his desk and write, or drink until he could no longer stay awake. Except for these times, he lived a quiet, untroubled life.

TAKATSUKI had landed the job he had always wanted—reporting for a top newspaper. Since he never studied, his grades at university were nothing to brag about, but the impression he made at interviews was overwhelmingly positive, and he had pretty much been hired on the spot. Sayoko had entered graduate school, as planned. Life was all smooth sailing for them. They married six months after graduation, the ceremony as cheerful and busy as Takatsuki himself. They honeymooned in France, and bought a two-room condo a short commute from downtown Tokyo. Junpei would come over for dinner a couple of times a week, and the newlyweds always welcomed him warmly. It was almost as if they were more comfortable with Junpei around than when they were alone.

Takatsuki enjoyed his work at the newspaper. They assigned him first to the city desk and kept him running around from one scene of tragedy to the next, in the course of which he saw many dead bodies. "I can see a corpse now and not feel a thing," he said. Bodies severed by trains, charred in fires, discolored with age, the bloated cadavers of the drowned, shotgun victims with brains splattered, dismembered corpses with heads and arms sawed off. "Whatever distinguishes one lump of flesh from another when we're alive, we're all the same once we're dead," he said. "Just used-up shells."

Takatsuki was sometimes too busy to make it home until morning. Then Sayoko would call Junpei. She knew he was often up all night.

"Are you working? Can you talk?"

"Sure," he would say. "I'm not doing anything special."

They would discuss the books they had read, or things that had come up in their daily lives. Then they would talk about the old days, when they were all still free and wild and spontaneous. Conversations like that would inevitably bring back memories of the time when Junpei had held Sayoko in his arms: the smooth touch of her lips, the smell of her tears, the softness of her breasts against him, the transparent early autumn sunlight streaming onto the tatami floor of his apartment—these were never far from his thoughts.

Just after she turned thirty, Sayoko became pregnant. She was a graduate assistant at the time, but she took a break from her job to have a baby. The three of them came up with names, but they settled in the end on Junpei's suggestion—"Sala." "I love the sound of it," Sayoko told him. There were no complications with the birth, and that night Junpei and Takatsuki found themselves together without Sayoko for the first time in a long while. Junpei had brought over a bottle of single malt to celebrate, and they emptied it together at the kitchen table.

"Why does time shoot by like this?" Takatsuki said with a depth of feeling that was rare for him. "It seems like only yesterday I was a freshman, and then I met you, and then Sayoko, and the next thing I know I'm a father. It's weird, like I'm watching a movie in fast-forward. But you wouldn't understand, Junpei. You're still living the same way you did in college. It's like you never stopped being a student, you lucky bastard."

"Not so lucky," Junpei said, but he knew how Takatsuki felt. Sayoko was a mother now. It was as big a shock for Junpei as it was for Takatsuki. The gears of life had moved ahead a notch with a loud *ker-chunk*, and Junpei knew that they would never turn back again. The one thing he was not yet sure of was how he ought to feel about it.

"I couldn't tell you this before," Takatsuki said, "but I'm sure Sayoko was more attracted to you than she was to me." He was pretty drunk, but there was a far more serious gleam in his eye than usual.

"That's crazy," Junpei said with a smile.

"Like hell it is. I know what I'm talking about. You know how to put pretty words on a page, but you don't know shit about a woman's feelings. A drowned corpse does better than you. You had no idea how she felt about you, but I figured, what the hell, I was in love with her, and I couldn't find anybody better, so I had to have her. I still think she's the greatest woman in the world. And I still think it was my right to have her."

"Nobody's saying it wasn't," Junpei said.

Takatsuki nodded. "But you *still* don't get it. Not really. 'Cause you're so damned *stupid*. That's OK, though. I don't care if you're stupid. You're not such a bad guy. I mean, look, you're the guy that gave my daughter her *name*."

"Yeah, OK, OK," Junpei said, "but I still don't *get* it when it comes to anything important."

"Exactly. When it comes to anything halfway important, you just don't *get* it. It's amazing to me that you can put a piece of fiction together."

"Yeah, well, that's a whole different thing."

"Anyhow, now there's four of us," Takatsuki said with a kind of sigh. "I wonder, though. Four of us. Four. Can that number be right?"

2

JUNPEI learned just before Sala's second birthday that Takatsuki and Sayoko were on the verge of breaking up. Sayoko seemed somewhat apologetic when she divulged the news to him. Takatsuki had had a lover since the time of Sayoko's pregnancy, she said, and he hardly ever came home anymore. It was someone he knew from work.

Junpei could not grasp what he was hearing, no matter how many details Sayoko was able to give him. Why did Takatsuki have to find himself another woman? He had declared Sayoko to be the greatest woman in the world the night Sala was born, and those words had come from deep in his gut. Besides, he was crazy about Sala. Why, in spite of that, did he have to abandon his family?

"I mean, I'm over at your house all the time, eating dinner with you guys, right? But I never sensed a thing. You were happiness itself—the perfect family."

"It's true," Sayoko said with a gentle smile. "We weren't lying to you or putting on an act. But quite separately from that, he got himself a girlfriend, and we can never go back to what we had. So we decided to split up. Don't let it bother you too much. I'm sure things will work out better now, in a lot of different ways."

"In a lot of different ways," she had said. The world is full of incomprehensible words, thought Junpei.

Sayoko and Takatsuki were divorced some months later.

They concluded agreements on several specific issues without the slightest hang-up: no recriminations, no disputed claims. Takatsuki went to live with his girlfriend; he came to visit Sala once a week, and they all agreed that Junpei would try to be present at those times. "It would make things easier for both of us," Sayoko told Junpei. Easier? Junpei felt as if he had grown much older all of a sudden, though he had just turned thirty-three.

Sala called Takatsuki "Papa" and Junpei "Jun." The four of them were an odd pseudo-family. Whenever they got together, Takatsuki would be his usual talkative self, and Sayoko's behavior was perfectly natural, as though nothing had happened. If anything, she seemed even more natural than before in Junpei's eyes. Sala had no idea her parents were divorced. Junpei played his assigned role perfectly without the slightest objection. The three joked around as always and talked about the old days. The only thing that Junpei understood about all this was that it was something the three of them needed.

"Hey, Junpei, tell me," Takatsuki said one January night when the two of them were walking home, breath white in the chill air. "Do you have somebody you're planning to marry?"

"Not at the moment," Junpei said.

"No girlfriend?"

"Nope, guess not."

"Why don't you and Sayoko get together?"

Junpei squinted at Takatsuki as if at some too-bright object. "Why?" he asked.

"'Why'?! Whaddya mean 'why'? It's so obvious! If nothing else, you're the only man I'd want to be a father to Sala."

"Is that the only reason you think I ought to marry Sayoko?"

Takatsuki sighed and draped his thick arm around Junpei's shoulders.

"What's the matter? Don't you like the idea of marrying Sayoko? Or is it the thought of stepping in after me?"

"That's not the problem. I just wonder if you can make, like, some kind of deal. It's a question of *decency.*"

"This is no deal," Takatsuki said. "And it's got nothing to do with decency. You love Sayoko, right? You love Sala, too, right? That's the most important thing. I know you've got your own special hang-ups. Fine. I grant you that. But to me, it looks like you're trying to pull off your shorts without taking off your pants."

Junpei said nothing, and Takatsuki fell into an unusually long silence. Shoulder to shoulder, they walked down the road to the station, heaving white breath into the night.

"In any case," Junpei said, "you're an absolute idiot."

"I have to give you credit," Takatsuki said. "You're right on the mark. I don't deny it. I'm ruining my own life. But I'm telling you, Junpei, I couldn't help it. There was no way I could put a stop to it. I don't know any better than you do why it had to happen. There's no way to justify it, either. It just happened. And if not here and now, something like it would have happened sooner or later."

Junpei felt he had heard this speech before. "Do you remember what you said to me the night Sala was born? That Sayoko was the greatest woman in the world, that you could never find anyone to take her place."

"And it's still true. Nothing has changed where that's concerned. But that very fact can sometimes make things go bad."

"I don't know what you mean by that," Junpei said.

"And you never will," Takatsuki said with a shake of the head. He always had the last word.

TWO years went by. Sayoko never went back to teaching. Junpei got an editor friend of his to send her a piece to translate, and she carried the job off with a certain flair. She had a gift for languages, and she knew how to write. Her work was fast, careful, and efficient, and the editor was impressed enough to bring her a new piece the following month that involved substantial literary translation. The pay was not very good, but it added to what Takatsuki was sending and helped Sayoko and Sala to live comfortably.

They all went on meeting at least once a week, as they always had. Whenever urgent business kept Takatsuki away, Sayoko, Junpei, and Sala would eat together. The table was quiet without Takatsuki, and the conversation turned to oddly mundane matters. A stranger would have assumed that the three of them were just a typical family.

Junpei went on writing a steady stream of stories, bringing out his fourth collection, *Silent Moon*, when he turned thirty-five. It received one of the prizes reserved for established writers, and the title story was made into a movie. Junpei also produced a few volumes of music criticism, wrote a book on ornamental gardening, and translated a collection of John Updike's short stories. All were well received. He had developed his own personal style which enabled him to transform the most deeply reverberating sounds and the subtle gradations of light and color into concise, convincing prose. Securing his position as a writer little by little, he had developed a steady readership, and a fairly stable income.

He continued to think seriously about asking Sayoko to marry him. On more than one occasion, he kept himself awake all night thinking about it, and for a time he was unable to work. But still, he could not make up his mind. The more he thought about it, the more it seemed to him that his relationship with Sayoko had been consistently directed by others. His position was always passive. Takatsuki was the one who had picked the two of them out of his class and created the threesome. Then he had taken Sayoko, married her, fathered a child with her, and divorced her. And now Takatsuki was the one who was urging Junpei to marry her. Junpei loved Sayoko, of course. About that there was no question. And now was the perfect time for him to be united with her. She probably wouldn't turn him down. But Junpei couldn't help thinking that things were just a bit *too* perfect. What was there left for *him* to decide? And so he went on wondering. And not deciding. And then the earthquake struck.

JUNPEI was in Barcelona at the time, writing a story for an airline magazine. He returned to his hotel in the evening to find the TV news filled with images of whole city blocks of collapsed buildings and black clouds of smoke. It looked like the aftermath of an air raid. Because the announcer was speaking in Spanish, it took Junpei a while to realize what city he was looking at, but it had to be Kobe. Several familiar-looking sights caught his eye. The expressway through Ashiya had collapsed. "You're from Kobe, aren't you?" his photographer asked.

"You're damn right I am," Junpei said.

But Junpei did not try to call his parents. The rift was too deep, and had gone on too long for there to be any hope of reconciliation. He flew back to Tokyo and resumed his normal life. He never turned on the television, and hardly looked at a newspaper. Whenever anyone mentioned the earthquake, he would clam up. It was an echo from a past that he had buried long ago. He hadn't set foot on those streets since his graduation, but still, the sight of the destruction laid bare raw wounds hidden somewhere deep inside him. The lethal, gigantic catastrophe seemed to change certain aspects of his life—quietly, but from the ground up. Junpei felt an entirely new sense of isolation. I have no roots, he thought. I'm not connected to anything.

Early on the Sunday morning that they had all planned to take Sala to the zoo to see the bears, Takatsuki called to say that he had to fly to Okinawa. He had managed at last to pry the promise of an hour-long one-on-one interview out of the governor. "Sorry, but you'll have to go to the zoo without me. I don't suppose Mr. Bear will be too upset if I don't make it."

So Junpei and Sayoko took Sala to the Ueno Zoo. Junpei held Sala in his arms and showed her the bears. She pointed to the biggest, blackest bear and asked, "Is that one Masakichi?"

"No no, that's not Masakichi," Junpei said. "Masakichi is smaller than that, and he's smarter-looking, too. That's the tough guy, Tonkichi."

"Tonkichi!" Sala yelled again and again, but the bear paid no attention. Then she looked at Junpei and said, "Tell me a story about Tonkichi."

"That's a hard one," Junpei said. "There aren't that many interesting stories about Tonkichi. He's just an ordinary bear. He can't talk or count money like Masakichi."

"But I bet you can tell me *something* good about him. One thing."

"You're absolutely right," Junpei said. "There's at least one good thing to tell about even the most ordinary bear. Oh yeah, I almost forgot. Well, Tonchiki—"

"Ton*ki*chi!" Sala corrected him with a touch of impatience.

"Ah yes, sorry. Well, Tonkichi had one thing he could do really well, and that was catching salmon. He'd go to the river and crouch down behind a boulder and—*snap!*—he would grab himself a salmon. You have to be really fast to do something like that. Tonkichi wasn't the brightest bear on the mountain, but he could catch more salmon than any of the other bears. More than he could ever hope to eat. But he couldn't go to town to sell his extra salmon, because he didn't know how to talk."

"That's easy," Sala said. "All he had to do was trade his extra salmon for Masakichi's extra honey."

"You're right," Junpei said. "And that's what Tonkichi decided to do. You and he had exactly the same idea. So Tonkichi and Masakichi started trading salmon for honey, and before long they got to know each other really well. Tonkichi realized that Masakichi was not such a stuck-up bear after all, and Masakichi realized that Tonkichi was not just a tough guy. Before they knew it, they were best friends. They talked about *everything*. They traded know-how. They told each other jokes. Tonkichi worked hard at catching salmon, and Masakichi worked hard at collecting honey. But then one day, like a bolt from the blue, the salmon disappeared from the river."

"A bolt from the blue?"

"Like a flash of lightning from a clear blue sky," Sayoko explained. "All of a sudden, without warning."

"All of a sudden the salmon disappeared?" Sala asked with a somber expression. "But why?"

"Well, all the salmon in the world got together and decided they weren't going to swim up that river anymore, because a bear named Tonkichi was there, and he was so good at catching salmon. Tonkichi never caught another salmon after that. The best he could do was catch an occasional skinny frog and eat it, but the worst-tasting thing you could ever want to eat is a skinny frog."

"Poor Tonkichi!" Sala said.

"And that's how Tonkichi ended up being sent to the zoo?" Sayoko asked.

"Well, that's a long, long story," Junpei said, clearing his throat. "But basically, yes, that's what happened."

"Didn't Masakichi help Tonkichi?" Sala asked.

"He tried, of course. They were best friends, after all. That's what friends are for. Masakichi shared his honey with Tonkichi—for free! But Tonkichi said, 'I can't let you do that. It'd be like taking advantage of you.' Masakichi said, 'You don't have to be such a stranger with me, Tonkichi. If I were in your position, you'd do the same thing for me, I'm sure. You would, wouldn't you?' "

"Sure he would," Sala said.

"But things didn't stay that way between them for long," Sayoko interjected.

"Things didn't stay that way between them for long," Junpei said. "Tonkichi told Masakichi, 'We're supposed to be friends. It's not right for one friend to do all the giving and the other to do all the taking: that's not real friendship. I'm leaving this mountain now, Masakichi, and I'll try my luck somewhere else. And if you and I meet up again somewhere, we can be best friends again.' So they shook hands and parted. But after Tonkichi got down from the mountain, he didn't know enough to be careful in the outside world, so a hunter caught him in a trap. That was the end of Tonkichi's freedom. They sent him to the zoo."

"Poor Tonkichi," Sala said.

"Couldn't you have come up with a better ending? Like, everybody lives happily ever after?" Sayoko asked Junpei later.

"I haven't thought of one yet."

THE three of them had dinner together as usual in Sayoko's apartment. Humming the "Trout," Sayoko boiled a pot of spaghetti and defrosted some tomato sauce while Junpei made a salad of green beans and onions. They opened a bottle of red wine and poured Sala a glass of orange juice. When they had finished eating and cleaning up, Junpei read to Sala from another picture book, but when bedtime came, she resisted.

"Please, Mommy, do the bra trick," she begged.

Sayoko blushed. "Not *now,*" she said. "We have a *guest.*"

"No we don't," Sala said. "Junpei's not a guest."

"What's this all about?" Junpei asked.

"It's just a silly game," Sayoko said.

"Mommy takes her bra off under her clothes, puts it on the table, and puts it back on again. She has to keep one hand on the table. And we time her. She's great!"

"Sala!" Sayoko growled, shaking her head. "It's just a little game we play at home. It's not meant for anybody else."

"Sounds like fun to me," Junpei said.

"Please, Mommy, show Junpei. Just once. If you do it, I'll go to bed right away."

"Oh, what's the use," Sayoko muttered. She took off her digital watch and handed it to Sala. "Now, you're not going to give me any more trouble about going to bed, right? OK, get ready to time me when I count to three."

Sayoko was wearing a baggy black crewneck sweater.

She put both hands on the table and counted, "One . . . two . . . *three!*" Like a turtle pulling into its shell, she slipped her right hand up inside her sleeve, and then there was a light back-scratching kind of movement. Out came the right hand again, and the left hand went up its sleeve. Sayoko turned her head just a bit, and the left hand came out holding a white bra—a small one with no wires. Without the slightest wasted motion, the hand and bra went back up the sleeve, and the hand came out again. Then the right hand pulled in, poked around at the back, and came out again. The end. Sayoko rested her right hand on her left on the table.

"Twenty-five seconds," Sala said. "That's great, Mommy, a new record! Your best time so far was thirty-six seconds."

Junpei applauded. "Wonderful! Like magic."

Sala clapped her hands, too. Sayoko stood up and announced, "All right, show time is over. To bed, young lady. You promised."

Sala kissed Junpei on the cheek and went to bed.

SAYOKO stayed with her until her breathing was deep and steady, then rejoined Junpei on the sofa. "I have a confession to make," she said. "I cheated."

"Cheated?"

"I didn't put the bra back on. I just pretended. I slipped it out from under my sweater and dropped it on the floor."

Junpei laughed. "What a terrible mother!"

"I wanted to make a new record," she said, narrowing her eyes with a smile. He hadn't seen her smile in that simple, natural way for a long time. Time wobbled on its axis inside him, like curtains stirring in a breeze. He reached for Sayoko's shoulder, and her hand took his. They came together on the sofa in a powerful embrace. With complete naturalness, they wrapped their arms around each other and kissed. It was as if nothing had changed since the time they were nineteen. Sayoko's lips had the same sweet fragrance.

"We should have been like this to begin with," she whispered after they had moved from the sofa to her bed. "But you didn't get it. You just didn't get it. Not till the salmon disappeared from the river."

They took off their clothes and held each other gently. Their hands groped clumsily, as if they were having sex for the first time in their lives. They took their time, until they knew they were ready, and then at last he entered Sayoko and she drew him in.

None of this seemed real to Junpei. In the half-light, he felt as if he were crossing a deserted bridge that went on and on forever. He moved, and she moved with him. Again and again he wanted to come, but he held back, fearing that, once it happened, the dream would end and everything would vanish.

Then, behind him, he heard a slight creaking sound.

The bedroom door was easing open. The light from the hallway took the shape of the door and fell on the rumpled bedclothes. Junpei raised himself and turned to see Sala standing against the light. Sayoko held her breath and moved her hips away, pulling him out. Gathering the sheets to her breast, she used one hand to straighten her hair.

Sala was not crying or screaming. Her right hand gripping the doorknob, she just stood there, looking at the two of them but seeing nothing, her eyes focused on emptiness.

Sayoko called her name.

"The man told me to come here," Sala said in a flat voice, like someone who has just been ripped out of a dream.

"The man?" Sayoko asked.

"The Earthquake Man. He came and woke me up. He told me to tell you. He said he has the box ready for everybody. He said he's waiting with the lid open. He said I should tell you that, and you'd understand."

SALA slept in Sayoko's bed that night. Junpei stretched out on the living room sofa with a blanket, but he could not sleep. The TV faced the sofa, and for a very long time he stared at the dead screen. *They* were inside there. They were waiting with the box open. He felt a chill run up his spine, and no matter how long he waited, it would not go away.

He gave up trying to sleep and went to the kitchen. He made himself some coffee and sat at the table to drink it, but he felt something bunched up under one foot. It was Sayoko's bra. He picked it up and hung it on the back of a chair. It was a simple, lifeless piece of white underwear, not particularly big. It hung over the kitchen chair in the predawn darkness like some anonymous witness who had wandered in from a time long past.

He thought about his early days in college. He could still hear Takatsuki the first time they met in class saying, "Hey, let's get something to eat," in that warm way of his, and he could see Takatsuki's friendly smile that seemed to say, *Hey, relax. The world is just going to keep getting better and better.* Where did we eat that time? Junpei wondered, and what did we have? He couldn't remember, though he was sure it was nothing special.

"Why did you choose me to go to lunch with?" Junpei had asked him that day. Takatsuki smiled and tapped his temple with complete confidence. "I have a talent for picking the right friends at the right times in the right place."

He was right, Junpei thought, setting his coffee mug on the kitchen table. Takatsuki *did* have an intuitive knack for picking the right friends. But that was not enough. Finding one person to love over the long haul of one's life was quite a different matter from finding friends. Junpei closed his eyes and thought about the long stretch of time that had passed through him. He did not want to think of it as something he had merely used up without any meaning.

As soon as Sayoko woke in the morning, he would ask her to marry him. He was sure now. He couldn't waste another minute. Taking care not to make a sound, he opened the bedroom door and looked at Sayoko and Sala sleeping bundled in a comforter. Sala lay with her back to Sayoko, whose arm was draped on Sala's shoulder. He touched Sayoko's hair where it fell across the pillow, and caressed Sala's small pink cheek with the tip of his finger. Neither of them stirred. He eased himself down to the carpeted floor by the bed, his back against the wall, to watch over them in their sleep.

Eyes fixed on the hands of the wall clock, Junpei thought about the rest of the story for Sala—the tale of Masakichi and Tonkichi. He had to find a way out. He couldn't just leave Tonkichi stranded in the zoo. He had to save him. He retraced the story from the beginning. Before long, the vague outline of an idea began to sprout in his head, and, little by little, it took shape.

Tonkichi had the same thought as Sala: he would use the honey that Masakichi had collected to bake honey pies. It didn't take him long to realize that he had a real talent for making crisp, delicious honey pies. Masakichi took the honey pies to town and sold them to the people there. The people loved Tonkichi's pies and bought them by the dozen. So Tonkichi and Masakichi never had to separate again: they lived happily ever after in the mountains, best friends forever.

SALA would be sure to love the new ending. And so would Sayoko.

I want to write stories that are different from the ones I've written so far, Junpei thought: I want to write about people who dream and wait for the night to end, who long for the light so they can hold the ones they love. But right now I have to stay here and keep watch over this woman and this girl. I will never let anyone—not anyone—try to put them into that crazy box—not even if the sky should fall or the earth crack open with a roar.

—*Translated by Jay Rubin*

LIEUTENANT MAMIYA'S LONG STORY: PART I

from THE WIND-UP BIRD CHRONICLE

I was shipped to Manchuria at the beginning of 1937, Lieutenant Mamiya began. I was a brand-new second lieutenant then, and they assigned me to the Kwantung Army General Staff in Hsin-ching. Geography had been my major in college, so I ended up in the Military Survey Corps, which specialized in mapmaking. This was ideal for me because, to be quite honest, the duties I was ordered to perform were among the easiest that anyone could hope for in the army.

In addition to this, conditions in Manchuria were relatively peaceful—or at least stable. The recent outbreak of the China Incident had moved the theater of military operations from Manchuria into China proper. The China Expeditionary Forces were the ones doing the actual fighting now, while the Kwantung Army had an easy time of it. True, mopping-up operations were still going on against anti-Japanese guerrilla units, but they were confined to the interior, and in general the worst was over. All that the powerful Kwantung Army had to do was police our newly "independent" puppet state of Manchukuo while keeping an eye on the north.

As peaceful as things supposedly were, it was still war, after all, so there were constant maneuvers. I didn't have to participate in those, either, fortunately. They took place under terrible conditions. The temperature would drop to forty or fifty degrees below zero. One false step in maneuvers like that, and you could end up dead. Every single time they held such maneuvers, there would be hundreds of men in the hospital with frostbite or sent to a hot spring for treatment. Hsin-ching was no big city, but it was certainly an exotic foreign place, and if you wanted to have fun there, it provided plenty of opportunities. New single officers like me lived together in a kind of rooming house rather than in barracks. It was more like an extension of student life. I took it easy, thinking that I would have nothing to complain about if my military service ended like this, just one peaceful day after another.

It was, of course, a make-believe peace. Just beyond the edges of our little circle of sunshine, a ferocious war was going on. Most Japanese realized that the war with China would turn into a muddy swamp from which we could never extricate ourselves, I believe—or at least any Japanese with a brain in his head realized this. It didn't matter how many local battles we won: there was no way Japan could continue to occupy and rule over such a huge country. It was obvious if you thought about it. And sure enough, as the fighting continued, the number of dead and wounded began to multiply. Relations with America went from bad to worse. Even at home, the shadows of war grew darker with every passing day. Those were dark years then: 1937, 1938. But living the easy life of an officer in Hsin-ching, you almost wanted to ask, "War? What war?" We'd go out drinking and carousing every night, and we'd visit the cafés that had the White Russian girls.

Then, one day late in April 1938, a senior officer of the general staff called me in and introduced me to a fellow in mufti named Yamamoto. He wore his hair short and had a mustache. He was not a very tall man. As for his age, I'd say he was in his mid-thirties. He had a scar on the back of his neck that looked as if it might have been made by a blade of some kind. The officer said to me: "Mr. Yamamoto is a civilian. He's been hired by the army to investigate the life and customs of the Mongolians who live in Manchukuo. He will next be going to the Hulunbuir Steppe, near the Outer Mongolian border, and we are going to supply him with an armed escort. You will be a member of that detachment." I didn't believe a thing he was telling me. This Yamamoto fellow might have been wearing civilian clothes, but anybody could tell at a glance that he was a professional soldier. The look in his eyes, the way he spoke, his posture: it was obvious. I figured he was a high-ranking officer or had something to do with intelligence and was on a mission that required him to conceal his military identity. There was something ominous about the whole thing.

Three of us were assigned to accompany Yamamoto—too few for an effective armed escort, though a larger group would have attracted the attention of the Outer Mongolian troops deployed along the border. One might have chosen to view this as a case of entrusting a sensitive mission to a few handpicked men, but the truth was far from that. I was the only officer, and I had zero battlefield experience. The only one we could count on for fighting power was a sergeant by the name of Hamano. I knew him well, as a soldier who had been assigned to assist the general staff. He was a tough fellow who had worked his way up through the ranks to become a noncommissioned officer, and he had distinguished himself in battle in China. He was big and fearless, and I was sure we could count on him in a pinch. Why they had also included Corporal Honda in our party I had no idea. Like me, he had just arrived from home, and of course he had no experience on the battlefield. He was a gentle, quiet soul who looked as if he would be no help at all in a fight. What's more, he belonged to the Seventh Division, which meant that the general staff had gone out of their way to have him sent over to us specifically for this assignment. That's how valuable a soldier he was, though not until much later did the reason for this become clear.

I was chosen to be the commanding officer of the escort because my primary responsibility was the topography of the western border of Manchukuo in the area of the Khalkha River. My job was to make sure that our maps of the district were as complete as possible. I had even been over the area several times in a plane. My presence was meant to help the mission go smoothly. My second assignment was to gather more detailed topographical information on the district and so increase the precision of our maps. Two birds with one stone, as it were. To be quite honest, the maps we had in those days of the Hulunbuir Steppe border region with Outer Mongolia were crude things—hardly an improvement over the old Manchu dynasty maps. The Kwantung Army had done several surveys following the establishment of Manchukuo. They wanted to make more accurate maps, but the area they had to cover was huge, and western Manchuria is just an endless desert. National borders don't mean very much in such a vast wilderness. The Mongolian nomads had lived there for thousands of years without the need—or even the concept—of borders.

The political situation had also delayed the making of more accurate maps. Which is to say that if we had gone ahead and unilaterally made an official map showing our idea of the border, it could have caused a full-scale international incident. Both the Soviet Union and Outer Mongolia, which shared borders with Manchukuo, were extremely sensitive about border violations, and there had been several instances of bloody combat over just such matters. In our day, the army was in no mood for war with the Soviet Union. All our force was invested in the war with China, with none to spare for a large-scale clash with the Soviets. We didn't have the divisions or the tanks or the artillery or the planes. The first priority was to secure the stability of Manchukuo, which was still a relatively new political entity. Establishment of the northern and northwestern borders could wait, as far as the army was concerned. They wanted to stall for time by keeping things indefinite. Even the mighty Kwantung Army deferred to this view and adopted a wait-and-see attitude. As a result, everything had been allowed to drift in a sea of vagueness.

If, however, their best-laid plans notwithstanding, some unforeseen event should lead to war (which is exactly what did happen the following year at Nomonhan), we would need maps to fight. And not just ordinary civilian maps, but real combat maps. To fight a war you need maps that show you where to establish encampments, the most effective place to set up your artillery, how many days it will take your infantry to march there, where to secure water, how much feed you need for your horses: a great deal of detailed information. You simply couldn't fight a modern war without such maps. Which is why much of our work overlapped with the work of the intelligence division, and we were constantly exchanging information with the Kwantung Army's intelligence section or the military secret service in Hailar. Everyone knew everyone else, but this Yamamoto fellow was someone I had never seen before.

After five days of preparation, we left Hsin-ching for Hailar by train. We took a truck from there, drove it through the area of the Khandur-byo Lamaist temple, and arrived at the Manchukuo Army's border observation post near the Khalkha River. I don't remember the exact distance, but it was something like two hundred miles. The region was an empty wilderness, with literally nothing as far as the eye could see. My work required me to keep checking my map against the actual landforms, but there was nothing out there for me to check against, nothing that one could call a landmark. All I could see were shaggy, grass-covered mounds stretching on and on, the unbroken horizon, and clouds floating in the sky. There was no way I could have any precise idea where on the map we were. All I could do was guess according to the amount of time we had been driving.

Sometimes, when one is moving silently through such an utterly desolate landscape, an overwhelming hallucination can make one feel that oneself, as an individual human being, is slowly coming unraveled. The surrounding space is so vast that it becomes increasingly difficult to keep a balanced grip on one's own being. I wonder if I am making myself clear. The mind swells out to fill the entire landscape, becoming so diffuse in the process that one loses the ability to keep it fastened to the physical self. That is what I experienced in the midst of the Mongolian steppe. How vast it was! It felt more like an ocean than a desert landscape. The sun would rise from the eastern horizon, cut its way across the empty sky, and sink below the western horizon. This was the only perceptible change in our surroundings. And in the movement of the sun, I felt something I hardly know how to name: some huge, cosmic love.

At the border post of the Manchukuo Army, we transferred from truck to horseback. They had everything ready for us there: four horses to ride, plus two packhorses loaded with food, water, and weapons. We were lightly armed. I and the man called Yamamoto carried only pistols. Hamano and Honda carried Model 38 regulation infantry rifles and two hand grenades each, in addition to their pistols.

The de facto commander of our group was Yamamoto. He made all the decisions and gave us instructions. Since he was supposedly a civilian, military rules required that I act as commanding officer, but no one doubted that he was the one in charge. He was simply that kind of man, for one thing, and although I held the rank of second lieutenant, I was nothing but a pencil pusher without battle experience. Military men can see who holds actual power, and that is the one they obey. Besides, my superiors had ordered me to follow Yamamoto's instructions without question. My obedience to him was to be something that transcended the usual laws and regulations.

We proceeded to the Khalkha River and followed it to the south. The river was swollen with snowmelt. We could see large fish in the water. Sometimes, in the distance, we spotted wolves. They might have been part wild dog rather than purebred wolves, but in any case they were dangerous. We had to post a sentry each night to guard the horses from them. We also saw a lot of birds, most of them migratory fowl on their way back to Siberia. Yamamoto and I discussed features of the topography. Checking our route against the map, we kept detailed notes on every bit of information that came to our notice. Aside from these technical exchanges, however, Yamamoto hardly ever spoke to me. He spurred his horse on in silence, ate away from the rest of us, and went to sleep without a word. I had the impression that this was not his first trip to the area. He had amazingly precise knowledge of the landforms, directions, and so forth.

After we had proceeded southward for two days without incident, Yamamoto called me aside and told me that we would be fording the Khalkha before dawn the next morning. This came as a tremendous shock to me. The opposite shore was Outer Mongolian territory. Even the bank on which we stood was a dangerous area of border disputes. The Outer Mongolians laid claim to it, and Manchukuo asserted its own claims to the territory, which had led to continual armed clashes. If we were ever taken prisoner by Outer Mongolian troops on this side, the differing views of the two countries gave us some excuse for being there, though in fact there was little danger of encountering them in this season, when snowmelt made fording so difficult. The far bank was a different story altogether. Mongolian patrols were over there for certain. If we were captured there, we would have no excuse whatever. It would be a clear case of border violation, which could stir up all kinds of political problems. We could be shot on the spot, and our government would be unable to protest. In addition, my superior officer had given me no indication that it would be all right for us to cross the border. I *had*, of course, been told to follow Yamamoto's orders, but I had no way of knowing if this included such a grave offense as a border violation. Secondly, as I said earlier, the Khalkha was quite swollen, and the current was far too strong to make a crossing, in addition to which the water must have been freezing cold. Not even the nomadic tribes wanted to ford the river at this time of year. They usually restricted their crossings to winter, when the river was frozen, or summer, when the flow was down and the water temperature up.

When I said all this to him, Yamamoto stared at me for a moment. Then he nodded several times. "I understand your concern about the violation of international borders," he said to me, with a somewhat patronizing air. "It is entirely natural for you, as an officer with men under your command, to consider the locus of responsibility in such a matter. You would never want to put the lives of your men in danger without good cause. But I want you to leave such questions to me. I will assume all responsibility in this instance. I am not in a position to explain a great deal to you, but this matter has been cleared with the highest levels of the army. As regards the fording of the river, we have no technical obstacles. There is a hidden point at which it is possible to cross. The Outer Mongolian Army has constructed and secured several such points. I suspect that you are fully aware of this as well. I myself have crossed the river a number of times at this point. I entered Outer Mongolia last year at this time at this same place. There is nothing for you to worry about."

He was right about one thing. The Outer Mongolian Army, which knew this area in detail, had sent combat units—though just a few of them—across to this side of the river during the season of melting snow. They had made sure they could send whole units across at will. And if *they* could cross, then this man called Yamamoto could cross, and it would not be impossible for the rest of us to cross too.

We stood now at one of those secret fords that had most likely been built by the Outer Mongolian Army. Carefully camouflaged, it would not have been obvious to the casual observer. A plank bridge, held in place by ropes against the swift current, connected the shallows on either side beneath the surface of the water. A slight drop in the water level would make for an easy crossing by troop transport vehicles, armored cars, and such. Reconnaissance planes could never spot it underwater. We made our way across the river's strong flow by clinging to the ropes. Yamamoto went first, to be certain there were no Outer Mongolian patrols in the area, and we followed. Our feet went numb in the cold water, but we and our horses struggled across to the far shore of the Khalkha River. The land rose up much higher on the far side, and standing there, we could see for miles across the desert expanse from which we had come. This was one reason the Soviet Army would always be in the more advantageous position when the battle for Nomonhan eventually broke out. The difference in elevation would also make for a huge difference in the accuracy of artillery fire. In any case, I remember being struck by how different the view was on either side of the river. I remember, too, how long it took to regain feeling in limbs that had been soaked in the icy water. I couldn't even get my voice to work for a while. But to be quite honest, the sheer tension that came from knowing I was in enemy territory was enough to make me forget about the cold.

We followed the river southward. Like an undulating snake, the Khalkha flowed on below us to the left. Shortly after the crossing, Yamamoto advised us to remove all insignia of rank, and we did as we were told. Such things could only cause trouble if we were captured by the enemy, I assumed. For this reason, I also removed my officer's boots and changed into gaiters.

We were setting up camp that evening when a man approached us from the distance, riding alone. He was a Mongol. The Mongols use an unusually high saddle, which makes it easy to distinguish them from afar. Sergeant Hamano snapped up his rifle when he saw the figure approaching, but Yamamoto told him not to shoot. Hamano slowly lowered his rifle without a word. The four of us stood there, waiting for the man to draw closer. He had a Soviet-made rifle strapped to his back and a Mauser at his waist. Whiskers covered his face, and he wore a hat with earflaps. His filthy robes were the same kind as the nomads', but you could tell from the way he handled himself that he was a professional soldier.

Dismounting, the man spoke to Yamamoto in what I assumed was Mongolian. I had some knowledge of both

Russian and Chinese, and what he spoke was neither of those, so it must have been Mongolian. Yamamoto answered in the man's own language. This made me surer than ever that Yamamoto was an intelligence officer.

Yamamoto said to me, "Lieutenant Mamiya, I will be leaving with this man. I don't know how long I will be away, but I want you to wait here—posting a sentry at all times, of course. If I am not back in thirty-six hours, you are to report that fact to headquarters. Send one man back across the river to the Manchukuo Army observation post." He mounted his horse and rode off with the Mongol, heading west.

The three of us finished setting up camp and ate a simple dinner. We couldn't cook or build a campfire. On that vast steppe, with nothing but low sand dunes to shield our presence as far as the eye could see, the least puff of smoke would have led to our immediate capture. We pitched our tents low in the shelter of the dunes, and for supper we ate dry crackers and cold canned meat. Darkness swiftly covered us when the sun sank beneath the horizon, and the sky was filled with an incredible number of stars. Mixed in with the roar of the Khalkha River, the sound of wolves howling came to us as we lay atop the sand, recovering from the day's exertions.

Sergeant Hamano said to me, "Looks like a tough spot we've got ourselves in," and I had to agree with him. By then, the three of us—Sergeant Hamano, Corporal Honda, and I—had gotten to know each other pretty well. Ordinarily, a fresh young officer like me would be kept at arm's length and laughed at by a seasoned noncommissioned officer like Sergeant Hamano, but our case was different. He respected the education I had received in a nonmilitary college, and I took care to acknowledge his combat experience and practical judgment without letting rank get in the way. We also found it easy to talk to each other because he was from Yamaguchi and I was from an area of Hiroshima close to Yamaguchi. He told me about the war in China. He was a soldier all the way, with only grammar school behind him, but he had his own reservations about this messy war on the continent, which looked as if it would never end, and he expressed these feelings honestly to me. "I don't mind fighting," he said. "I'm a soldier. And I don't mind dying in battle for my country, because that's my job. But this war we're fighting now, Lieutenant—well, it's just not right. It's not a real war, with a battle line where you face the enemy and fight to the finish. We advance, and the enemy runs away without fighting. Then the Chinese soldiers take their uniforms off and mix with the civilian population, and we don't even know who the enemy *is.* So then we kill a lot of innocent people in the name of flushing out 'renegades' or 'remnant troops,' and we commandeer provisions. We have to steal their food, because the line moves forward so fast our supplies can't catch up with us. And we have to kill our prisoners, because we don't have anyplace to keep them or any food to feed them. It's wrong, Lieutenant. We did some terrible things in Nanking. My own unit did. We threw dozens of people into a well and dropped hand grenades in after them. Some of the things we did I couldn't bring myself to talk about. I'm telling you, Lieutenant, this is one war that doesn't have any Righteous Cause. It's just two sides killing each other. And the ones who get stepped on are the poor farmers, the ones without politics or ideology. For them, there's no Nationalist Party, no Young Marshal Zhang, no Eighth Route Army. If they can eat, they're happy. I know how these people feel: I'm the son of a poor fisherman myself. The little people slave away from morning to night, and the best they can do is keep themselves alive—just barely. I can't believe that killing these people for no reason at all is going to do Japan one bit of good."

In contrast to Sergeant Hamano, Corporal Honda had very little to say about himself. He was a quiet fellow, in any case. He'd mostly listen to us talk, without injecting his own comments. But while I say he was "quiet," I don't mean to imply there was anything dark or melancholy about him. It's just that he rarely took the initiative in a conversation. True, that often made me wonder what was on his mind, but there was nothing unpleasant about him. If anything, there was something in his quiet manner that softened people's hearts. He was utterly serene. He wore the same look on his face no matter what happened. I gathered he was from Asahikawa, where his father ran a small print shop. He was two years younger than I, and from the time he left middle school he had joined his brothers, working for his father. He was the youngest of three boys, the eldest of whom had been killed in China two years earlier. He loved to read, and whenever we had a spare moment, you'd see him curled up somewhere, reading a book on some kind of Buddhist topic.

As I said earlier, Honda had absolutely no combat experience, but with only one year of training behind him, he was an outstanding soldier. There are always one or two such men in any platoon, who, patient and enduring, carry out their duties to the letter without a word of complaint. Physically strong, with good intuition, they instantly grasp what you tell them and get the job done right. Honda was one of those. And because he had had cavalry training, he was the one who knew the most about horses; he took care of the six we had with us. And he did this in an extraordinary way. It sometimes seemed to us that he understood every little thing the horses were feeling. Sergeant Hamano acknowledged Corporal Honda's abilities immediately and let him take charge of many things without the slightest hesitation.

So, then, for such an oddly patched-together unit, we attained an extraordinarily high degree of mutual understanding. And precisely because we were not a regular unit, we had none of that by-the-book military formality.

We were so at ease with one another, it was almost as if Karma had brought us together. Which is why Sergeant Hamano was able to say openly to me things that lay far beyond the fixed framework of officer and noncom.

"Tell me, Lieutenant," he once asked, "what do you think of this fellow Yamamoto?"

"Secret service, I'm willing to bet," I said. "Anybody who can speak Mongol like that has got to be a pro. And he knows this area like the back of his hand."

"That's what I think. At first I thought he might be one of those mounted bandits connected with top brass, but that can't be it. I know those guys. They'll talk your ear off and make up half of what they tell you. And they're quick on the trigger. But this Yamamoto guy's no lightweight. He's got guts. He *is* brass—and way up there. I can smell 'em a mile away. I heard something about some kind of secret tactical unit the army's trying to put together with Mongols from Soviet-trained troops, and that they brought over a few of our pros to run the operation. He could be connected with that."

Corporal Honda was standing sentry a little ways away from us, holding his rifle. I had my Browning lying close by, where I could grab it at any time. Sergeant Hamano had taken his gaiters off and was massaging his feet.

"I'm just guessing, of course," Hamano went on. "That Mongol we saw could be some anti-Soviet officer with the Outer Mongolian Army, trying to make secret contact with the Japanese Army."

"Could be," I said. "But you'd better watch what you say. They'll have your head."

"Come on, Lieutenant. I'm not that stupid. This is just between us." He flashed me a big smile, then turned serious. "But if any of this is true, it's risky business. It could mean war."

I nodded in agreement. Outer Mongolia was supposedly an independent country, but it was actually more of a satellite state under the thumb of the Soviet Union. In other words, it wasn't much different from Manchukuo, where Japan held the reins of power. It did have an anti-Soviet faction, though, as everyone knew, and through secret contacts with the Japanese Army in Manchukuo, members of that faction had fomented a number of uprisings. The nucleus of the insurgent element consisted of Mongolian Army men who resented the high-handedness of the Soviet military, members of the landowning class opposed to the forced centralization of the farming industry, and priests of the Lama sect, who numbered over one hundred thousand. The only external power that the anti-Soviet faction could turn to for help was the Japanese Army stationed in Manchukuo. And they apparently felt closer to us Japanese, as fellow Asians, than they did to the Russians. Plans for a large-scale uprising had come to light in the capital city of Ulan Bator the previous year, 1937, and there had been a major purge carried out. Thousands of military men and Lamaist priests had been executed as counterrevolutionary elements in secret touch with the Japanese Army, but still anti-Soviet feeling continued to smolder in one place or another. So there would have been nothing strange about a Japanese intelligence officer crossing the Khalkha River and making secret contact with an anti-Soviet officer of the Outer Mongolian Army. To prevent such activities, the Outer Mongolian Army had guard units making constant rounds and had declared the entire band of territory ten to twenty kilometers in from the Manchukuo border to be off-limits, but this was a huge area to patrol, and they could not keep watch on every bit of it.

Even if their rebellion should succeed, it was obvious that the Soviet Army would intervene at once to crush their counterrevolutionary activity, and if that happened the insurgents would request the help of the Japanese Army, which would then give Japan's Kwantung Army an excuse to intervene. Taking Outer Mongolia would amount to sticking a knife in the guts of the Soviets' development of Siberia. Imperial Headquarters back in Tokyo might be trying to put the brakes on, but this was not an opportunity that the ambitious Kwantung Army General Staff was about to let slip from their fingers. The result would be no mere border dispute but a full-scale war between the Soviet Union and Japan. If such a war broke out on the Manchurian-Soviet border, Hitler might respond by invading Poland or Czechoslovakia. This was the situation that Sergeant Hamano had been referring to in his remark on the potential for war.

The sun rose the next morning, and still Yamamoto had not returned. I was the last one to stand sentry. I borrowed Sergeant Hamano's rifle, sat atop a somewhat higher sand dune, and watched the eastern sky. Dawn in Mongolia was an amazing thing. In one instant, the horizon became a faint line suspended in the darkness, and then the line was drawn upward, higher and higher. It was as if a giant hand had stretched down from the sky and slowly lifted the curtain of night from the face of the earth. It was a magnificent sight, far greater in scale, as I said earlier, than anything that I, with my limited human faculties, could fully comprehend. As I sat and watched, the feeling overtook me that my very life was slowly dwindling into nothingness. There was no trace here of anything as insignificant as human undertakings. This same event had been occurring hundreds of millions—hundreds of billions—of times, from an age long before there had been anything resembling life on earth. Forgetting that I was there to stand guard, I watched the dawning of the day, entranced.

After the sun rose fully above the horizon, I lit a cigarette, took a sip of water from my canteen, and urinated.

Then I thought about Japan. I pictured my hometown in early May—the fragrance of the flowers, the babbling of the river, the clouds in the sky. Friends from long ago. Family. The chewy sweetness of a warm rice puff wrapped in oak leaf. I'm not that fond of sweets, as a rule, but I can still remember how badly I wanted a *mochi* puff that morning. I would have given half a year's pay for one just then. And when I thought about Japan, I began to feel as if I had been abandoned at the edge of the world. Why did we have to risk our lives to fight for this barren piece of earth devoid of military or industrial value, this vast land where nothing lived but wisps of grass and biting insects? To protect my homeland, I too would fight and die. But it made no sense to me at all to sacrifice my one and only life for the sake of this desolate patch of soil from which no shaft of grain would ever spring.

YAMAMOTO came back at dawn the following day. I stood final watch that morning too. With the river at my back, I was staring toward the west when I heard what sounded like a horse's whinny behind me. I spun around but saw nothing. I stared toward where I had heard the sound, gun at the ready. I swallowed, and the sound from my own throat was loud enough to frighten me. My trigger finger was trembling. I had never once shot a gun at anyone.

But then, some seconds later, staggering over the crest

of a sand dune, came a horse bearing Yamamoto. I surveyed the area, finger still on the trigger, but no one else appeared—neither the Mongol who had come for him nor enemy soldiers. A large white moon hung in the eastern sky like some ill-omened megalith. Yamamoto's left arm seemed to have been wounded. The handkerchief he had wrapped around it was stained with blood. I woke Corporal Honda to see to the horse. Heavily lathered and breathing hard, it had obviously come a long way at high speed. Hamano stood sentry in my place, and I got the first-aid kit to treat Yamamoto's wound.

"The bullet passed through, and the bleeding stopped," said Yamamoto. He was right: the bullet had missed the bone and gone all the way through, tearing only the flesh in its path. I removed the handkerchief, disinfected the openings of the wound with alcohol, and tied on a new bandage. He never flinched the whole time, though his upper lip wore a thin film of sweat. He drank deeply from a canteen, lit a cigarette, and inhaled with obvious relish. Then he took out his Browning, wedged it under his arm, removed the clip, and with one hand deftly loaded three rounds into it. "We leave here right away, Lieutenant Mamiya," he said. "Cross the Khalkha and head for the Manchukuo Army observation post."

We broke camp quickly, with hardly a word among us, mounted the horses, and headed for the ford. I asked Yamamoto nothing about how he had been shot or by whom. I was not in a position to do so, and even if I had been, he probably wouldn't have told me. The only thought in my mind at the time was to get out of this enemy territory as quickly as possible, cross the Khalkha River, and reach the relative safety of the opposite bank.

We rode in silence, urging our horses across the grassy plain. No one spoke, but all were thinking the same thing: could we make it across that river? If an Outer Mongolian patrol reached the bridge before we did, it would be the end for us. There was no way we could win in a fight. I remember the sweat streaming under my arms. It never once dried.

"Tell me, Lieutenant Mamiya, have you ever been shot?" Yamamoto asked me after a long silence atop his horse.

"Never," I replied.

"Have you ever shot anyone?"

"Never," I said again.

I had no idea what kind of impression my answers made on him, nor did I know what his purpose was in asking me those questions.

"This contains a document that has to be delivered to headquarters," he said, placing his hand on his saddlebag. "If it can't be delivered, it has to be destroyed—burned, buried, it doesn't matter, but it must not, under any circumstances, be allowed to fall into enemy hands. *Under any circumstances.* That is our first priority. I want to be sure you understand this. It is *very, very* important."

"I understand," I said.

Yamamoto looked me in the eye. "If the situation looks bad, the first thing you have to do is shoot me. Without hesitation. If I can do it myself, I will. But with my arm like this, I may not be able to. In that case, you have to shoot me. And make sure you shoot to kill."

I nodded in silence.

WHEN we reached the ford, just before dusk, the fear that I had been feeling all along turned out to be all too well founded. A small detachment of Outer Mongolian troops was deployed there. Yamamoto and I climbed one of the higher dunes and took turns looking at them through the binoculars. There were eight men—not a lot, but for a border patrol they were heavily armed. One man carried a light machine gun, and there was one heavy machine gun, mounted on a rise. It was surrounded by sandbags and aimed at the river. They had obviously stationed themselves there to prevent us from crossing to the other bank. They had pitched their tents by the river and staked their ten horses nearby. It looked as if they were planning to stay in place until they caught us. "Isn't there another ford we could use?" I asked.

Yamamoto took his eyes from the binoculars and looked at me, shaking his head. "There is one, but it's too far. Two days on horseback. We don't have that much time. All we can do is cross here, whatever it takes."

"Meaning we ford at night?"

"Correct. It's the only way. We leave the horses here. We finish off the sentry, and the others will probably be asleep. Don't worry, the river will blot out most sounds. I'll take care of the sentry. There's nothing for us to do until then, so better get some sleep, rest ourselves now while we have the chance."

We set our fording operation for three in the morning. Corporal Honda took all the packs from the horses, drove the animals to a distant spot, and released them. We dug a deep hole and buried our extra ammunition and food. All that each of us would carry would be a canteen, a day's rations, a gun, and a few bullets. If we were caught by the Outer Mongolians, with their overwhelmingly superior firepower, we could never outfight them, no matter how much ammunition we might carry. Now the thing for us to do was to get what sleep we could, because if we did make it across the river, there would be no chance to sleep for some time. Corporal Honda would stand sentry first, with Sergeant Hamano taking his place.

Stretching out in the tent, Yamamoto fell asleep immediately. He apparently hadn't slept at all the whole time. By his pillow was a leather valise, into which he had transferred the important document. Hamano fell asleep soon after him. We were all exhausted, but I was too tense to sleep. I lay there for a long time, dying for sleep but kept awake by imagined scenes of us killing the sentry and being sprayed with machine gun fire as we forded the river. My palms were dripping with sweat, and my temples throbbed. I could not be sure that when the time came, I would be able to conduct myself in a manner befitting an officer. I crawled out of the tent and went to sit by Corporal Honda on sentry duty.

"You know, Honda," I said, "we're maybe going to die here."

"Hard to say," he replied.

For a while, neither of us said anything. But there was something in his answer that bothered me—a particular tone that contained a hint of uncertainty. Intuition has never been my strong suit, but I knew that his vague remark was intended to conceal something. I decided to question him about it. "If you have something to tell me, don't hold back now," I said. "This could be the last time we ever talk to each other, so open up."

Biting his lower lip, Honda stroked the sand at his feet. I could see he was wrestling with conflicting feelings. "Lieutenant," he said after some time had passed. He looked me straight in the eye. "Of the four of us here, you will live the longest—far longer than you yourself would imagine. You will die in Japan."

Now it was my turn to look at him. He continued:

"You may wonder how I know that, but it is something that not even I can explain. I just know."

"Are you psychic or something?"

"Maybe so, though the word doesn't quite seem to fit what I feel. It's a little too grandiose. Like I say, I just know, that's all."

"Have you always had this kind of thing?"

"Always," he said with conviction. "Though I've kept it hidden ever since I was old enough to realize what was happening. But this is a matter of life and death, Lieutenant, and *you* are the one who's asking me about it, so I'm telling you the truth."

"And how about other people? Do you know what's going to happen to them?"

He shook his head. "Some things I know, some things I don't know. But you'd probably be better off not knowing, Lieutenant. It may be presumptuous of someone like me to say such big-sounding things to a college graduate like you, but a person's destiny is something you look back at after it's passed, not something you see in advance. I have a certain amount of experience where these things are concerned. You don't."

"But anyhow, you say I'm not going to die here?"

He scooped up a handful of sand and let it run out between his fingers. "This much I can say, Lieutenant. You won't be dying here on the continent."

I wanted to go on talking about this, but Corporal Honda refused to say anything more. He seemed to be absorbed in his own contemplations or meditations. Holding his rifle, he stared out at the vast prairie. Nothing I said seemed to reach him.

I went back to the low-pitched tent in the shelter of a dune, lay down beside Sergeant Hamano, and closed my eyes. This time sleep came to take me—a deep sleep that all but pulled me by the ankles to the bottom of the sea.

—*Translated by Jay Rubin*

LIEUTENANT MAMIYA'S LONG STORY: PART II

from THE WIND-UP BIRD CHRONICLE

What woke me was the metallic click of a rifle's safety being released. No soldier in battle could ever miss that sound, even in a deep sleep. It's a—how can I say it?—a special sound, as cold and heavy as death itself. Almost instinctively, I reached for the Browning next to my pillow, but just then a shoe slammed into my temple, the impact blinding me momentarily. After I had brought my breathing under control, I opened my eyes just enough to see the man who must have kicked me. He was kneeling down and picking up my Browning. I slowly lifted my head, to find the muzzles of two rifles pointed at my face. Beyond the rifles stood two Mongolian soldiers.

I was sure I had fallen asleep in a tent, but the tent was gone now, and a skyful of stars shone overhead. Another Mongolian soldier was pointing a light machine gun at the head of Yamamoto, who was lying beside me. He lay utterly still, as if conserving his energy because he knew it was useless to resist. All of the Mongols wore long overcoats and battle helmets. Two of them were aiming large flashlights at Yamamoto and at me. At first I couldn't grasp what had happened: my sleep had been too deep and the shock too great. But the sight of the Mongolian soldiers and of Yamamoto's face left no doubt in my mind: our tents had been discovered before we had had a chance to ford the river.

Then it occurred to me to wonder what had become of Honda and Hamano. I turned my head very slowly, trying to survey the area, but neither man was there. Either they had been killed already or they had managed to escape.

These had to be the men of the patrol we had seen earlier at the ford. They were few in number, and they were equipped with a light machine gun and rifles. In command was a ruggedly built noncom, the only one of the bunch to be wearing proper military boots. He was the man who had kicked me. He bent over and picked up the leather valise that Yamamoto had had by his head. Opening it, he looked inside, then he turned it upside down and shook it. All that fell to the ground was a pack of cigarettes. I could hardly believe it. With my own eyes, I had seen Yamamoto putting the document into that bag. He had taken it from a saddlebag, put it in this valise, and placed the valise by his pillow. Yamamoto struggled to maintain his cool, but I saw his expression momentarily begin to change. He obviously had no idea what had happened to the document. But whatever the explanation might be, its disappearance must have been a great relief to him. As he had said to me earlier, our number one priority was seeing to it that the document never fell into enemy hands.

The soldiers dumped all our belongings on the ground and inspected them in detail, but they found nothing important. Next they stripped us and went through our pockets. They bayoneted our clothing and packs, but they found no documents. They took our cigarettes and pens, our wallets and notebooks and watches, and pocketed them. By turns, they tried on our shoes, and anyone they fit took them. The men's arguments over who got what became pretty intense, but the noncom ignored them. I suppose it was normal among the Mongols to take booty from prisoners of war and enemy dead. The noncom took only Yamamoto's watch, leaving the other items for his men to fight over. The rest of our equipment—our pistols and ammunition and maps and compasses and binoculars—went into a cloth bag, no doubt for sending to Ulan Bator headquarters.

Next they tied us up, naked, with strong, thin rope. At close range, the Mongol soldiers smelled like a stable that had not been cleaned for a long, long time. Their uniforms were shabby, filthy with mud and dust and food stains to the point where it was all but impossible to tell what the original color had been. Their shoes were full of holes and falling off their feet—quite literally. No wonder they wanted ours. They had brutish faces for the most part, their teeth a mess, their hair long and wild. They looked more like mounted bandits or highwaymen than soldiers, but their Soviet-made weapons and their starred insignia indicated that they were regular troops of the Mongolian People's Republic. To me, of course, their discipline as a fighting unit and their military esprit seemed rather poor. Mongols make for tough, long-suffering soldiers, but they're not much suited to modern group warfare.

The night was freezing cold. Watching the white clouds of the Mongolian soldiers' breath bloom and vanish in the darkness, I felt as if a strange error had brought me into the landscape of someone else's nightmare. I couldn't grasp that this was actually happening. It was indeed a nightmare, but only later did I come to realize that it was just the beginning of a nightmare of enormous proportions.

A short time later, one of the Mongolian soldiers came out of the darkness, dragging something heavy. With a big smile, he threw the object on the ground next to us. It was Hamano's corpse. The feet were bare: someone had already taken his boots. They proceeded to strip his clothes off, examining everything they could find in his pockets. Hands reached out for his watch, his wallet, and his cigarettes. They divided up the cigarettes and smoked them while looking through the wallet. This yielded a few pieces of Manchukuo paper money and a photo of a woman who was probably Hamano's mother. The officer in charge said something and took the money. The photo was flung to the ground.

One of the Mongolian soldiers must have sneaked up behind Hamano and slit his throat while he was standing guard. They had done to us first what we had been planning to do to them. Bright-red blood was flowing from the body's gaping wound, but for such a big wound there was not much blood; most of it had probably been lost by then. One of the soldiers pulled a knife from the scabbard on his belt, its curved blade some six inches long. He waved it in my face. I had never seen such an oddly shaped knife. It seemed to have been designed for some special purpose. The soldier made a throat-slashing motion with the knife and whistled through his teeth. Some of the others laughed. Rather than government issue, the knife seemed to be the man's personal property. Everyone had a long bayonet at his waist, but this man was the only one carrying a curved knife, and he had apparently used it to slit Hamano's throat. After a few deft swirls of the blade, he returned it to its scabbard.

Without a word, and moving only his eyes, Yamamoto

sent a glance in my direction. It lasted just an instant, but I knew immediately what he was trying to say: Do you think Corporal Honda managed to get away? Through all the confusion and terror, I had been thinking the same thing: Where *is* Corporal Honda? If Honda escaped this sudden attack of the Outer Mongolian troops, there might be some chance for us—a slim chance, perhaps, and the question of what Honda could do out there alone was depressing, but some chance was better than no chance at all.

They kept us tied up all night, lying on the sand. Two soldiers were left to watch over us: one with the light machine gun, the other with a rifle. The rest sat some distance away, smoking, talking, and laughing, seemingly relaxed now that they had captured us. Neither Yamamoto nor I said a word. The dawn temperature dropped to freezing in that place, even in May. I thought we might freeze to death, lying there naked. But the cold itself was nothing in comparison with the terror I felt. I had no idea what we were in for. These men were a simple patrol unit: they probably did not have the authority to decide what to do with us. They had to wait for orders. Which meant that we would probably not be killed right away. After that, however, there was no way to tell what would happen. Yamamoto was more than likely a spy, and I had been caught with him, so naturally I would be seen as an accomplice. In any case, we would not get off easily.

Some time after dawn broke, a sound like the drone of an airplane engine came out of the distant sky. Eventually, the silver-colored fuselage entered my field of vision. It was a Soviet-made reconnaissance plane, bearing the insignia of Outer Mongolia. The plane circled above us several times. The soldiers all waved, and the plane dipped its wing in return. Then it landed in a nearby open area, sending up clouds of sand. The earth was hard here, and there were no obstructions, which made it relatively easy to take off and land without a runway. For all I knew, they might have used the same spot for this purpose any number of times. One of the soldiers mounted a horse and galloped off toward the plane with two saddled horses in tow.

When they returned, the two horses carried men who appeared to be high-ranking officers. One was Russian, the other Mongolian. I assumed that the patrol had radioed headquarters about our capture and that the two officers had made the trip from Ulan Bator to interrogate us. They were intelligence officers, no doubt. I had heard that the GPU was at work behind the scenes in the previous year's mass arrest and purge of antigovernment activists.

Both officers wore immaculate uniforms and were clean-shaven. The Russian wore a kind of trench coat with a belt. His boots shone with an unblemished luster. He was a thin man, but not very tall for a Russian, and perhaps in his early thirties. He had a wide forehead, a narrow nose, and skin almost pale pink in color, and he wore wire-rim glasses. Overall, though, this was a face that made no impression to speak of. Standing next to him, the short, stout, dark Mongolian officer looked like a little bear.

The Mongolian called the noncom aside, and the three men talked for a while. I guessed that the officers were asking for a detailed report. The noncom brought over a bag containing the things they had confiscated from us and showed them to the others. The Russian studied each object with great care, then put them all back into the bag. He said something to the Mongolian, who in turn spoke to the noncom. Then the Russian took a cigarette case from his breast pocket and opened it for the other two. They went on talking and smoking together. Several times, as he spoke, the Russian slammed his right fist into his left palm. He looked somewhat annoyed. The Mongolian officer kept his arms folded and his face grim, while the noncom shook his head now and then.

Eventually, the Russian officer ambled over to where we lay on the ground. "Would you like a smoke?" he asked in Russian. As I said earlier, I had studied Russian in college and could follow a conversation pretty well, but I pretended not to understand, so as to avoid any difficulties. "Thanks, but no thanks," said Yamamoto in Russian. He was good.

"Excellent," said the Soviet Army officer. "Things will go more quickly if we can speak in Russian."

He removed his gloves and put them in his coat pocket. A small gold ring shone on his left hand. "As you are no doubt aware, we are looking for a certain something. Looking very hard for it. And we know you have it. Don't ask how we know; we just know. But you do not have it on you now. Which means that, logically speaking, you must have hidden it before you were captured. You haven't transported it over there." He motioned toward the Khalkha River. "None of you has crossed the river. The letter must be on this side, hidden somewhere. Do you understand what I have said to you so far?"

Yamamoto nodded. "I understand," he said, "but we know nothing about a letter."

"Fine," said the Russian, expressionless. "In that case, I have one little question to ask you. What were you men doing over here? As you know, this territory belongs to the Mongolian People's Republic. What was your purpose in entering land that belongs to others? I want to hear your reason for this."

"Mapmaking," Yamamoto explained. "I am a civilian employee of a map company, and this man and the one they killed were with me for protection. We knew that this side of the river was your territory, and we are sorry for having crossed the border, but we did not think of ourselves as having made a territorial violation. We simply wanted to observe the topography from the vantage point of the plateau on this side."

Far from amused, the Russian officer curled his lips into a smile. " 'We are sorry'?" he said slowly. "Yes, of course. You wanted to see the topography from the plateau. Yes, of course. The view is always better from high ground. It makes perfect sense."

For a time he said nothing, but stared at the clouds in the sky. Then he returned his gaze to Yamamoto, shook his head slowly, and sighed.

"If only I could believe what you are telling me! How much better it would be for all of us! If only I could pat you on the shoulder and say, 'Yes, yes, I see, now run along home across the river, and be more careful in the future.' I truly wish I could do this. But unfortunately, I cannot. Because I know who you are. And I know what you are doing here. We have friends in Hailar, just as you have friends in Ulan Bator."

He took the gloves from his pocket, refolded them, and put them back. "Quite honestly, I have no personal interest in hurting you or killing you. If you would simply give me the letter, then I would have no further business with you. You would be released from this place immediately at my discretion. You could cross the river and go home. I promise you that, on my honor. Anything else that happened would be an internal matter for us. It would have nothing to do with you."

The light of the sun from the east was finally beginning to warm my skin. There was no wind, and a few hard white clouds floated in the sky.

A long, long silence followed. No one said a word. The Russian officer, the Mongolian officer, the men of the patrol, and Yamamoto: each preserved his own sphere of silence. Yamamoto had seemed resigned to death from the moment of our capture; his face never showed the slightest hint of expression.

"The two of you . . . will . . . almost certainly . . . die here," the Russian went on slowly, a phrase at a time, as if speaking to children. "And it will be a terrible death. They . . ." And here the Russian glanced toward the Mongolian soldiers. The big one, holding the machine gun, looked at me with a snaggletoothed grin. "They love to kill people in ways that involve great difficulty and imagination. They are, shall we say, aficionados. Since the days of Genghis Khan, the Mongols have enjoyed devising particularly cruel ways to kill people. We Russians are painfully aware of this. It is part of our history lessons in school. We study what the Mongols did when they invaded Russia. They killed millions. For no reason at all. They captured hundreds of Russian aristocrats in Kiev and killed them all together. Do you know that story? They cut huge, thick planks, laid the Russians beneath them, and held a banquet on top of the planks, crushing them to death beneath their weight. Ordinary human beings would never think of such a thing, don't you agree? It took time and a tremendous amount of preparation. Who else would have gone to the trouble? But they did it. And why? Because it was a form of amusement to them. And they still enjoy doing such things. I saw them in action once. I thought I had seen some terrible things in my day, but that night, as you can imagine, I lost my appetite. Do you understand what I am saying to you? Am I speaking too quickly?"

Yamamoto shook his head.

"Excellent," said the Russian. He paused, clearing his throat. "Of course, this will be the second time for me. Perhaps my appetite will have returned by dinnertime. If possible, however, I would prefer to avoid unnecessary killing."

Hands clasped together behind his back, he looked up at the sky for a time. Then he took his gloves out and glanced toward the plane. "Beautiful weather," he said. "Spring. Still a little cold, but just about right. Any hotter, and there would be mosquitoes. Terrible mosquitoes. Yes, spring is much better than summer." He took out his cigarette case again, put a cigarette between his lips, and lit it with a match. Slowly, he drew the smoke into his lungs, and slowly he let it out again. "I'm going to ask you once more: Do you insist that you really know nothing about the letter?"

Yamamoto said only one word: *"Nyet."*

"Fine," said the Russian. "Fine." Then he said something in Mongolian to the Mongolian officer. The man nodded and barked an order to the soldiers. They carried over some rough logs and began to sharpen them with their bayonets, quickly turning them into four stakes. Pacing off the distance between the stakes, they pounded them into the ground with rocks at the four corners of a square. All these preparations took some twenty minutes to complete, I guessed, but I had absolutely no idea what they were for.

The Russian said, "To them, an excellent slaughter is like an excellent meal. The longer they take with their preparations, the more enjoyment they derive from the act. Simply killing a man is no problem: one pistol shot and it's all over. But that would not be"—and here he ran his fingertip slowly over his smooth chin—"very interesting."

They untied Yamamoto and led him to the staked-off area. There they tied his arms and legs to the four stakes. Stretched out on the ground, stark naked, Yamamoto had several raw wounds on his body.

"As you know, these people are shepherds," said the Russian officer. "And shepherds use their sheep in many ways: they eat their flesh, they shear their wool, they take their hides. To them, sheep are the perfect animal. They spend their days with sheep—their whole lives with sheep. They know how to skin them with amazing skill. The hides they use for tents and clothing. Have you ever seen them skin a sheep?"

"Just kill me and get it over with," said Yamamoto.

The Russian brought his palms together and, while rubbing them slowly, nodded to Yamamoto. "Don't worry," he said. "We will be certain to kill you. I guarantee you that. It may take a little time, but you will die. There is nothing to worry about on that score. We are in no hurry. Here we are in the vast wilderness, where there is nothing as far as the eye can see. Only time. All the time we need. And I have many things I wish to tell you. Now, as to the procedure of skinning: Every band has at least one specialist—one professional, as it were, who knows everything there is to know about cutting off the skin, a man of miraculous skill. His skinning is a work of art. He does it in the twinkling of an eye, with such speed and dexterity you would think that the creature being skinned alive never noticed what was happening. But of course"—he took the cigarette case from his breast pocket once again, shifted it to his left hand, and tapped upon it with the fingers of his right—"not to notice such a thing would be out of the question. The one being skinned alive experiences terrible pain. Unimaginable pain. And it takes an incredibly long time for death to come. Massive hemorrhaging is what does it finally, but that takes time."

He snapped his fingers. The Mongolian officer stepped forward. From his coat pocket he produced a sheathed knife. It was shaped like the one used before by the soldier who had made the throat-slitting gesture. He pulled the knife from its sheath and held it aloft. In the morning sun, the blade shone with a dull white gleam.

"This man is one of those professionals of whom I spoke," said the Russian officer. "I want you to look at his knife. Closely. It is a very special knife, designed for skinning, and it is extraordinarily well made. The blade is as thin and sharp as a razor. And the technical skill these people bring to the task is extremely high. They've been skinning animals for thousands of years, after all. They can take a man's skin off the way you'd peel a peach. Beautifully, without a single scratch. Am I speaking too quickly for you, by any chance?"

Yamamoto said nothing.

"They do a small area at a time," said the Russian officer. "They have to work slowly if they want to remove the skin cleanly, without any scratches. If, in the meantime, you feel you want to say something, please let me know. Then you won't have to die. Our man here has done this several times, and never once has he failed to make the person talk. Keep that in mind. The sooner we stop, the better for both of us."

Holding his knife, the bearlike Mongolian officer looked at Yamamoto and grinned. To this day, I remember that smile. I see it in my dreams. I have never been able to forget it. No sooner had he flashed this smile than he set to work. His men held Yamamoto down with their hands and knees while he began skinning Yamamoto with the utmost care. It truly was like skinning a peach. I couldn't bear to watch. I closed my eyes. When I did this, one of the soldiers hit me with his rifle butt. He went on hitting me until I opened my eyes. But it hardly mattered: eyes open or closed, I could still hear Yamamoto's voice. He bore the pain without a whimper—at first. But soon he began to scream. I had never heard such screams before: they did not seem part of this world. The man started by slitting open Yamamoto's shoulder and proceeded to peel off the skin of his right arm from the top down—slowly, carefully, almost lovingly. As the Russian officer had said, it was something like a work of art. One would never have imagined there was any pain involved, if it weren't for the screams. But the screams told the horrendousness of the pain that accompanied the work.

Before long, the entire skin of Yamamoto's right arm had come off in a single thin sheet. The skinner handed it to the man beside him, who held it open in his fingertips, circulating among the others to give them a good look. All the while, blood kept dripping from the skin. Then the officer turned to Yamamoto's left arm, repeating the procedure. After that he skinned both legs, cut off the penis and testicles, and removed the ears. Then he skinned the head and the face and everything else. Yamamoto lost consciousness, regained it, and lost it again. The screams would stop whenever he passed out and continue when he came to again. But his voice gradually weakened and finally gave out altogether. All this time, the Russian officer drew meaningless patterns on the ground with the heel of his boot. The Mongolian soldiers watched the procedure in silence. Their faces remained expressionless, showing neither disgust nor excitement nor shock. They watched Yamamoto's skin being removed a piece at a time with the same kind of faces we might have if we were out for a stroll and stopped to have a look at a construction site.

Meanwhile, I did nothing but vomit. Over and over again. Long after it seemed there was nothing more for me to bring up, I continued to vomit. At last, the bearlike Mongolian officer held up the skin of Yamamoto's torso, which he had so cleanly peeled off. Even the nipples were intact. Never to this day have I seen anything so horrible. Someone took the skin from him and spread it out to dry the way we might dry a sheet. All that remained lying on the ground was Yamamoto's corpse, a bloody red lump of meat from which every trace of skin had been removed. The most painful sight was the face. Two large white eyeballs stared out from the red mass of flesh. Teeth bared, the mouth stretched wide open as if in a shout. Two little holes were all that remained where the nose had been removed. The ground was a sea of blood.

The Russian officer spit on the ground and looked at

me. Then he took a handkerchief from his pocket and wiped his mouth. "The fellow really didn't know anything, did he?" he said, putting the handkerchief back. His voice sounded somewhat flatter than it had before. "If he had known, he would have talked. Pity. But in any case, the man was a professional. He was bound to have an ugly death sooner or later. Ah, well, can't be helped. And if *he* knew nothing, there's no way that you could know anything."

He put a cigarette between his lips and struck a match. "Which means that you are no longer of any use to us. Not worth torturing for information. Not worth keeping alive as a prisoner. We want to dispose of this affair in the utmost secrecy. There could be complications if we brought you back to Ulan Bator. The best thing, of course, would be to put a bullet in your brain here and now, then bury you or burn you and throw your ashes into the Khalkha. That would be a simple end to the matter. Don't you agree?" He fixed his eyes on mine. I continued to pretend that I could not understand him. "You don't understand Russian, I suppose. It's a waste of time to spell this out to you. Ah, well. I might as well be talking to myself. So hear me out. In any case, I have good news for you. I have decided not to kill you. Think of this as my own small expression of penitence for having pointlessly killed your friend in spite of myself. We've all had our fill of killing this morning. Once a day is more than enough. And so I will not kill you. Instead, I will give you a chance to survive. If all goes well, you may even come out of this alive. The chances of that happening are not good, of course. Perhaps nonexistent. But a chance is a chance. At least it is far better than being skinned alive. Don't you agree?"

He raised his hand and summoned the Mongolian officer. With great care, the man had been washing his knife with water from a canteen and had just finished sharpening it on a whetstone. The soldiers had laid out the pieces of Yamamoto's skin and were standing by them, discussing something. They seemed to be exchanging opinions on the finer points of the skinner's technique. The Mongolian officer put his knife in its scabbard and then into the pocket of his coat before approaching us. He looked me in the face for a moment, then turned to his fellow officer. The Russian spoke a few short Mongolian phrases to him, and without expression the man nodded. A soldier brought two horses for them.

"We'll be going back to Ulan Bator now," the Russian said to me. "I hate to return empty-handed, but it can't be helped. Win some, lose some. I hope my appetite comes back by dinnertime, but I rather doubt it will."

They mounted their horses and left. The plane took off, became a silver speck in the western sky, then disappeared altogether, leaving me alone with the Mongolian soldiers and their horses.

They set me on a horse and lashed me to the saddle. Then, in formation, we moved out to the north. The soldier just in front of me kept singing some monotonous melody in a voice that was barely audible. Aside from that, there was nothing to be heard but the dry sound of the horses' hooves kicking up sand. I had no idea where they were taking me or what they were going to do to me. All I knew was that to them, I was a superfluous being of no value whatever. Over and over in my head I repeated to myself the words of the Russian officer. He had said he would not kill me. He would not kill me, but my chances of surviving were almost nonexistent. What could this mean? It was too vague for me to grasp in any concrete way. Perhaps they were going to use me in some kind of horrible game. They wouldn't simply dispatch me, because they planned to enjoy the dreadful contrivance at their leisure.

But at least they hadn't killed me. At least they hadn't skinned me alive like Yamamoto. I might not be able to avoid being killed in the end, but not like *that.* I was alive for now; I was still breathing. And if what the Russian officer had said was true, I would not be killed immediately. The more time that lay between me and death, the more chance I had to survive. It might be a minuscule chance, but all I could do was cling to it.

Then, all of a sudden, the words of Corporal Honda flared to life again in my brain: that strange prognostication of his that I would not die on the continent. Even as I sat there, tied to the saddle, the skin of my naked back burning in the desert sun, I repeatedly savored every syllable that he had spoken. I let myself dwell on his expression, his intonation, the sound of each word. And I resolved to believe him from the bottom of my heart. No, no, I was not going to lie down and die in a place like this! I would come out of this alive! I would tread my native soil once again!

We traveled north for two hours or more, coming to a stop near a Lamaist devotional mound. These stone markers, called *oboo,* serve both as the guardian deity for travelers and as valuable signposts in the desert. Here the men dismounted and untied my ropes. Supporting my weight from either side, two of them led me a short distance away. I figured that this was where I would be killed. A well had been dug into the earth here. The mouth of the well was surrounded by a three-foot-high stone curb. They made me kneel down beside it, grabbed my neck from behind, and forced me to look inside. I couldn't see a thing in the solid darkness. The noncom with the boots found a fist-sized rock and dropped it into the well. Some time later came the dry sound of stone hitting sand. So the well was a dry one, apparently. It had once served as a well in the desert, but it must have dried up long before, owing to a movement of the subterranean vein of water.

Judging from the time it took the stone to hit bottom, it seemed to be fairly deep.

The noncom looked at me with a big grin. Then he took a large automatic pistol from the leather holster on his belt. He released the safety and fed a bullet into the chamber with a loud click. Then he put the muzzle of the gun against my head.

He held it there for a long time but did not pull the trigger. Then he slowly lowered the gun and raised his left hand, pointing toward the well. Licking my dry lips, I stared at the gun in his fist. What he was trying to tell me was this: I had a choice between two fates. I could have him shoot me now—just die and get it over with. Or I could jump into the well. Because it was so deep, if I landed badly I might be killed. If not, I would die slowly at the bottom of a dark hole. It finally dawned on me that this was the chance the Russian officer had spoken of. The Mongolian noncom pointed at the watch that he had taken from Yamamoto and held up five fingers. He was giving me five seconds to decide. When he got to three, I stepped onto the well curb and leaped inside. I had no choice. I had hoped to be able to cling to the wall and work my way down, but he gave me no time for that. My hands missed the wall, and I tumbled down.

It seemed to take a very long time for me to hit bottom. In reality, it could not have been more than a few seconds, but I do recall thinking about a great many things on my way down. I thought about my hometown, so far away. I thought about the girl I slept with just once before they shipped me out. I thought about my parents. I recall feeling grateful that I had a younger sister and not a brother: even if I was killed, they would still have her and not have to worry about her being taken by the army. I thought about rice cakes wrapped in oak leaves. Then I slammed into dry ground and lost consciousness for a moment. It felt as if all the air inside me had burst through the walls of my body. I thudded against the well bottom like a sandbag.

It truly was just a moment that I lost consciousness from the impact, I believe. When I came to, I felt some kind of spray hitting me. At first I thought it was rain, but I was wrong. It was urine. The Mongolian soldiers were all peeing on me where I lay in the bottom of the well. I looked up to see them in silhouette far above me, taking turns coming to the edge of the round hole to pee. There was a terrible unreality to the sight, like a drug-induced hallucination. But it was real. I was really in the bottom of the well, and they were spraying me with real pee. Once they had finished, someone shone a flashlight on me. I heard them laughing. And then they disappeared from the edge of the hole. After that, everything sank into a deep silence.

For a while, I thought it best to lie there facedown,

waiting to see if they would come back. But after twenty minutes had gone by, then thirty (as far as I could tell without a watch), they did not come back. They had gone away and left me, it seemed. I had been abandoned at the bottom of a well in the middle of the desert. Once it was clear that they would not be returning, I decided to check myself over for injuries. In the darkness, this was no easy feat. I couldn't see my own body. I couldn't tell with my own eyes what condition it was in. I could only resort to my perceptions, but I could not be sure that the perceptions I was experiencing in the darkness were accurate. I felt that I was being deceived, deluded. It was a very strange feeling.

Little by little, though, and with great attention to detail, I began to grasp my situation., The first thing I realized was that I had been extremely lucky. The bottom of the well was relatively soft and sandy. If it hadn't been, then the impact of falling such a distance would have broken every bone in my body. I took one long, deep breath and tried to move. First I tried moving my fingers. They responded, although somewhat feebly. Then I tried to raise myself to a sitting position on the earthen surface, but this I was unable to do. My body felt as if it had lost all sensation. My mind was fully conscious, but there was something wrong with the connection between my mind and my body. My mind would decide to do something, but it was unable to convert the thought into muscular activity. I gave up and, for a while, lay there quietly in the dark.

Just how long I remained still I have no idea. But little by little, my perceptions began to return. And along with the recovery of my perceptions, naturally enough, came the sensation of pain. Intense pain. Almost certainly, my leg was broken. And my shoulder might be dislocated or, perhaps, if luck was against me, even broken.

I lay still, enduring the pain. Before I knew it, tears were streaming down my cheeks—tears of pain and, even more, tears of despair. I don't think you will ever be able to understand what it is like—the utter loneliness, the feeling of desperation—to be abandoned in a deep well in the middle of the desert at the edge of the world, overcome with intense pain in total darkness. I went so far as to regret that the Mongolian noncom had not simply shot me and gotten it over with. If I had been killed that way, at least they would have been aware of my death. If I died here, however, it would be a truly lonely death, a death of no concern to anyone, a silent death.

Now and then, I heard the sound of the wind. As it moved across the surface of the earth, the wind made an uncanny sound at the mouth of the well, a sound like the moan of a woman in tears in a far-off world. That world and this were joined by a narrow shaft, through which the woman's voice reached me here, though only at long, irregular intervals. I had been left all alone in deep silence and even deeper darkness.

Enduring the pain, I reached out to touch the earthen floor around me. The well bottom was flat. It was not very wide, maybe five or five and a half feet. As I was groping the ground, my hand suddenly came upon a hard, sharp object. In reflexive fear, I drew my hand back, but then slowly and carefully I reached out toward the thing. Again my fingers came in contact with the sharp object. At first I thought it was a tree branch, but soon enough I realized I was touching bones. Not human bones, but those of a small animal, which had been scattered at random, either by the passage of time or by my fall. There was nothing else at the bottom of the well, just sand: fine and dry.

Next I ran my palm over the wall. It seemed to be made of thin, flat stones. As hot as the desert surface became in daytime, that heat did not penetrate to this world belowground. The stones had an icy chill to them. I ran my hand over the wall, examining the gaps between stones. If I could get a foothold there, I might be able to climb to the surface. But the gaps turned out to be too narrow for that, and in my battered state, climbing seemed all but impossible.

With a tremendous effort, I dragged myself closer to the wall and raised myself against it, into a sitting position. Every move made my leg and shoulder throb as if they had been stuck with hundreds of thick needles. For a while after that, each breath made me feel that my body might crack apart. I touched my shoulder and realized it was hot and swollen.

HOW much time went by after that I do not know. But at one point something happened that I would never have imagined. The light of the sun shot down from the opening of the well like some kind of revelation. In that instant, I could see everything around me. The well was filled with brilliant light. A flood of light. The brightness was almost stifling: I could hardly breathe. The darkness and cold were swept away in a moment, and warm, gentle sunlight enveloped my naked body. Even the pain I was feeling seemed to be blessed by the light of the sun, which now warmly illuminated the white bones of the small animal beside me. These bones, which could have been an omen of my own impending fate, seemed in the sunlight more like a comforting companion. I could see the stone walls that encircled me. As long as I remained in the light, I was able to forget about my fear and pain and despair. I sat in the dazzling light in blank amazement. Then the light disappeared as suddenly as it had come. Deep darkness covered everything once again. The whole interval had been extremely short. In terms of the clock, it must have lasted ten or, at the most, fifteen seconds. No doubt, because of the angles involved, this was all the sun could manage to shine straight down to the bottom of the hole in any single day. The flood of sunlight was gone before I could begin to comprehend its meaning.

After the light faded, I found myself in an even deeper darkness than before. I was all but unable to move. I had no water, no food, not a scrap of clothing on my body. The long afternoon went by, and night came, when the temperature plunged. I could hardly sleep. My body craved sleep, but the cold pricked my skin like a thousand tiny thorns. I felt as if my life's core was stiffening and dying bit by bit. Above me, I could see stars frozen in the sky. Terrifying numbers of stars. I stared up at them, watching as they slowly crept along. Their movement helped me ascertain that time was continuing to flow on. I slept for a short while, awoke with the cold and pain, slept a little more, then woke again.

Eventually, morning came. From the round mouth of the well, the sharp pinpoints of starlight gradually began to fade. Still, even after dawn broke, the stars did not disappear completely. Faint almost to the point of imperceptibility, they continued to linger there, on and on. To slake my thirst, I licked the morning dew that clung to the stone wall. The amount of water was minuscule, of course, but to me it tasted like a bounty from heaven. The thought crossed my mind that I had had neither food nor water for an entire day. And yet I had no sense of hunger.

I remained there, still, in the bottom of the hole. It was all I could do. I couldn't even think, so profound were my feelings of loneliness and despair. I sat there doing nothing, thinking nothing. Unconsciously, however, I waited for that ray of light, that blinding flood of sunlight that poured straight down to the bottom of the well for one tiny fraction of the day. It must have been a phenomenon that occurred very close to noon, when the sun was at the highest point in the sky and its light struck the surface of the earth at right angles. I waited for the coming of the light and for nothing else. There was nothing else I could wait for.

A very long time went by, it seems. At some point I drifted into sleep. By the time I sensed the presence of something and woke, the light was already there. I realized that I was being enveloped once again by that overwhelming light. Almost unconsciously, I spread open both my hands and received the sun in my palms. It was far stronger than it had been the first time. And it lasted far longer than it had then. At least it felt that way to me. In the light, tears poured out of me. I felt as if all the fluids of my body might turn into tears and come streaming from my eyes, that my body itself might melt away like this. If it could have happened in the bliss of this marvelous light, even death would have been no threat. Indeed, I felt I *wanted* to die. I had a marvelous sense of oneness, an overwhelming sense of unity. Yes, that was it: the true meaning of life resided in that light that lasted for however many seconds it was, and I felt I *ought to die* right then and there.

But of course, before anything could happen, the light was gone. I was still there, in the bottom of that miserable well. Darkness and cold reasserted their grip on me, as if to declare that the light had never existed at all. For a long time, I simply remained huddled where I was, my face bathed in tears. As if beaten down by some huge power, I was unable to do—or even to think—anything at all, unable to feel even my own physical existence. I was a dried-up carcass, the cast-off shell of an insect. But then, once again, into the empty room of my mind, returned the prophecy of Corporal Honda: I would not die on the continent. Now, after the light had come and gone, I found myself able to believe his prophecy. I could believe it now because, in a place where I should have died, and at a time when I should have died, I had been unable to die. It was not that I *would not* die: I *could not* die. Do you understand what I am saying, Mr. Okada? Whatever heavenly grace I may have enjoyed until that moment was lost forever.

AT this point in his story, Lieutenant Mamiya looked at his watch. "And as you can see," he added softly, "here I am." He shook his head as if trying to sweep away the invisible threads of memory. "Just as Mr. Honda had said, I did not die on the continent. And of the four of us who went there, I have lived the longest."

I nodded in response.

"Please forgive me for talking on at such length. It must have been very boring for you, listening to a useless old man chatter on about the old days." Lieutenant Mamiya shifted his position on the sofa. "My goodness, I'll be late for my train if I stay any longer."

I hastened to restrain him. "Please don't end your story there," I said. "What happened after that? I want to hear the rest."

He looked at me for a moment.

"How would this be, then?" he asked. "I really am running late, so why don't you walk with me to the bus stop? I can probably give you a quick summary along the way."

I left the house with him and walked to the bus stop.

"On the third morning, I was saved by Corporal Honda. He had sensed that the Mongols were coming for us that night, slipped out of the tent, and remained in hiding all that time. He had taken the document from Yamamoto's bag with him. He did this because our number one priority was to see to it that the document not fall into enemy hands, no matter how great the sacrifice we had to make. No doubt you are wondering why, if he realized that the Mongols were coming, Corporal Honda ran away by himself instead of waking the rest of us so that we could escape together. The simple fact of the matter is that we had no hope of winning in such a situation. They knew that we were there. It was their territory. They had us far outnumbered and outgunned. It would have been the simplest thing in the world for them to find us, kill us, and take the document. Given the situation, Corporal Honda had no choice but to escape by himself. On the battlefield, his actions would have been a clear case of deserting under fire, but on a special assignment like ours, the most important thing is resourcefulness.

"He saw everything that happened. He watched them skinning Yamamoto. He saw the Mongolian soldiers take me away. But he no longer had a horse, so he could not follow immediately. He had to come on foot. He dug up the extra supplies that we had buried in the desert, and there he buried the document. Then he came after me. For him to find me down in the well, though, required a tremendous effort. He didn't even know which direction we had taken."

"How *did* he find the well?" I asked.

"I don't know," said Lieutenant Mamiya. "He didn't say much about that. He *just knew,* I'd say. When he found me, he tore his clothing into strips and made a long rope. By then, I was practically unconscious, which made it all the more difficult for him to pull me up. Then he managed to find a horse and put me on it. He took me across the dunes, across the river, and to the Manchukuo Army outpost. There they treated my wounds and put me on a truck sent out by headquarters. I was taken to the hospital in Hailar."

"What ever happened to that document or letter or whatever it was?"

"It's probably still there, sleeping in the earth near the Khalkha River. For Corporal Honda and me to go all the way back and dig it up would have been out of the question, nor could we find any reason to make such an effort. We arrived at the conclusion that such a thing should never have existed in the first place. We coordinated our stories for the army's investigation. We decided to insist that we had heard nothing about any document. Otherwise, they probably would have held us responsible for not bringing it back from the desert. They kept us in separate rooms, under strict guard, supposedly for medical treatment, and they questioned us every day. All these high-ranking officers would come and make us tell our stories over and over again. Their questions were meticulous, and very clever. But they seemed to believe us. I told them every little detail of what I had experienced, being careful to omit anything I knew about the document.

Once they got it all down, they warned me that this was a top-secret matter that would not appear in the army's formal records, that I was never to mention it to anyone, and that I would be severely punished if I did. Two weeks later, I was sent back to my original post, and I believe that Corporal Honda was also returned to his home unit."

"One thing is still not clear to me," I said. "Why did they go to all the trouble of bringing Mr. Honda from his unit for this assignment?"

"He never said much to me about that. He had probably been forbidden to tell anyone, and I suspect that he thought it would be better for me not to know. Judging from my conversations with him, though, I imagine there was some kind of personal relationship between him and the man they called Yamamoto, something that had to do with his special powers. I had often heard that the army had a unit devoted to the study of the occult. They supposedly gathered people with these spiritual or psychokinetic powers from all over the country and conducted experiments on them. I suspect that Mr. Honda met Yamamoto in that connection. In any case, without those powers of his, Mr. Honda would never have been able to find me in the well and guide me to the exact location of the Manchukuo Army outpost. He had neither map nor compass, yet he was able to head us straight there without the slightest uncertainty. Common sense would have told you that such a thing was impossible. I was a professional mapmaker, and I knew the geography of that area quite well, but I could never have done what he did. These powers of Mr. Honda were probably what Yamamoto was looking to him for."

We reached the bus stop and waited.

"Certain things will always remain as riddles, of course," said Lieutenant Mamiya. "There are many things I still don't understand. I still wonder who that lone Mongolian officer was who met us in the desert. And I wonder what would have happened if we had managed to bring that document back to headquarters. Why did Yamamoto not simply leave us on the right bank of the Khalkha and cross over by himself? He would have been able to move around far more freely that way. Perhaps he had been planning to use us as a decoy for the Mongolian troops so that he could escape alone. It certainly is conceivable. Perhaps Corporal Honda realized this from the start and that was why he merely stood by while the Mongolians killed him.

"In any case, it was a very long time after that before Corporal Honda and I had an opportunity to meet again. We were separated from the moment we arrived in Hailar and were forbidden to speak or even to see each other. I had wanted to thank him one last time, but they made that impossible. He was wounded in the battle for Nomonhan and sent home, while I remained in Manchuria until the end of the war, after which I was sent to Siberia. I was only able to find him several years later, after I was repatriated from my Siberian internment. We did manage to meet a few times after that, and we corresponded. But he seemed to avoid talking about what had happened to us at the Khalkha River, and I myself was not too eager to discuss it. For both of us, it had simply been too enormous an experience. We shared it by *not talking about it.* Does this make any sense?

"This has turned into a very long story, but what I wanted to convey to you was my feeling that real life may have ended for me deep in that well in the desert of Outer Mongolia. I feel as if, in the intense light that shone for a mere ten or fifteen seconds a day in the bottom of the well, I burned up the very core of my life, until there was nothing left. That is how mysterious that light was to me. I can't explain it very well, but as honestly and simply as I can state it, no matter what I have encountered, no matter what I have experienced since then, I ceased to feel anything in the bottom of my heart. Even in the face of those monstrous Soviet tank units, even when I lost this left hand of mine, even in the hellish Soviet internment camps, a kind of numbness was all I felt. It may sound strange to say this, but none of that mattered. Something inside me was already dead. Perhaps, as I felt at the time, I should have died in that light, simply faded away. That was the time for me to die. But, as Mr. Honda had predicted, I did not die there. Or perhaps I should say that I *could not* die there.

"I came back to Japan, having lost my hand and twelve precious years. By the time I arrived in Hiroshima, my parents and my sister were long since dead. They had put my little sister to work in a factory, which was where she was when the bomb fell. My father was on his way to see her at the time, and he, too, lost his life. The shock sent my mother to her deathbed; she finally passed away in 1947. As I told you earlier, the girl to whom I had been secretly engaged was now married to another man, and she had given birth to two children. In the cemetery, I found my own grave. There was nothing left for me. I felt truly empty, and knew that I should not have come back there. I hardly remember what my life has been like since then. I became a social studies teacher and taught geography and history in high school, but I was not, in the true sense of the word, alive. I simply performed the mundane tasks that were handed to me, one after another. I never had one real friend, no human ties with the students in my charge. I never loved anyone. I no longer knew what it meant to love another person. I would close my eyes and see Yamamoto being skinned alive. I dreamed about it over and over. Again and again I watched them peel the skin off and turn him into a lump of flesh. I could hear his heartrending screams. I also had dreams of myself slowly rotting away, alive, in the bottom of the well. Sometimes it seemed to me that that was what had really happened and that my life here was the dream.

"When Mr. Honda told me on the bank of the Khalkha River that I would not die on the continent, I was overjoyed. It was not a matter of believing or not believing: I wanted to cling to something then—anything at all. Mr. Honda probably knew that and told me what he did in order to comfort me. But of joy there was to be none for me. After returning to Japan, I lived like an empty shell. Living like an empty shell is not really living, no matter how many years it may go on. The heart and flesh of an empty shell give birth to nothing more than the life of an empty shell. This is what I hope I have made clear to you, Mr. Okada."

"Does this mean," I ventured, "that you never married after returning to Japan?"

"Of course not," answered Lieutenant Mamiya. "I have no wife, no parents or siblings. I am entirely alone."

After hesitating a moment, I asked, "Are you sorry that you ever heard Mr. Honda's prediction?"

Now it was Lieutenant Mamiya's turn to hesitate. After a moment of silence, he looked me straight in the face. "Maybe I am," he said. "Maybe he should never have spoken those words. Maybe I should never have heard them. As Mr. Honda said at the time, a person's destiny is something you look back at afterward, not something to be known in advance. I do believe this, however: now it makes no difference either way. All I am doing now is fulfilling my obligation to go on living."

The bus came, and Lieutenant Mamiya favored me with a deep bow. Then he apologized to me for having taken up my valuable time. "Well, then, I shall be on my way," he said. "Thank you for everything. I am glad in any case that I was able to hand you the package from Mr. Honda. This means that my job is done at last. I can go home with an easy mind." Using both his right hand and the artificial one, he deftly produced the necessary coins and dropped them into the fare box.

I stood there and watched as the bus disappeared around the next corner. After it was gone, I felt a strange emptiness inside, a hopeless kind of feeling like that of a small child who has been left alone in an unfamiliar neighborhood.

Then I went home, and sitting on the living room couch, I opened the package that Mr. Honda had left me as a keepsake. I worked up a sweat removing layer after layer of carefully sealed wrapping paper, until a sturdy cardboard box emerged. It was a fancy Cutty Sark gift box, but it was too light to contain a bottle of whiskey. I opened it, to find nothing inside. It was absolutely empty. All that Mr. Honda had left me was an empty box.

—*Translated by Jay Rubin*

ICE MAN

I married an ice man.

I first met him in a hotel at a ski resort, which is probably the perfect place to meet an ice man. The hotel lobby was crowded with animated young people, but the ice man was sitting by himself on a chair in the corner farthest from the fireplace, quietly reading a book. Although it was nearly noon, the clear, chilly light of an early-winter morning seemed to linger around him.

"Look, that's an ice man," my friend whispered.

At the time, though, I had absolutely no idea what an ice man was. My friend didn't, either. "He must be made of ice. That's why they call him an ice man." She said this to me with a serious expression, as if she were talking about a ghost or someone with a contagious disease.

The ice man was tall, and he seemed to be young, but

his stubby, wirelike hair had patches of white in it, like pockets of unmelted snow. His cheekbones stood out sharply, like frozen stone, and his fingers were rimed with a white frost that looked as if it would never melt. Otherwise, though, the ice man seemed like an ordinary man. He wasn't what you'd call handsome, but you could see that he might be very attractive, depending on how you looked at him. In any case, something about him pierced me to the heart, and I felt this, more than anywhere, in his eyes. His gaze was as silent and transparent as the splinters of light that pass through icicles on a winter morning. It was like the single glint of life in an artificial body.

I stood there for a while and watched the ice man from a distance. He didn't look up. He just sat without moving, reading his book as though there were no one else around him.

THE next morning, the ice man was in the same place again, reading a book in exactly the same way. When I went to the dining room for lunch, and when I came back from skiing with my friends that evening, he was still there, directing the same gaze onto the pages of the same book. The same thing happened the day after that. Even when the sun sank low, and the hour grew late, he sat in his chair, as quiet as the winter scene outside the window.

On the afternoon of the fourth day, I made up some

excuse not to go out on the slopes. I stayed in the hotel by myself and loitered for a while in the lobby, which was as empty as a ghost town. The air there was warm and moist, and the room had a strangely dejected smell—the smell of snow that had been tracked in on the soles of people's shoes and was now melting in front of the fireplace. I looked out the windows, rustled through the pages of a newspaper or two, and then went over to the ice man, gathered my nerve, and spoke.

I tend to be shy with strangers and, unless I have a very good reason, I don't usually talk to people I don't know. But I felt compelled to talk to the ice man no matter what. It was my last night at the hotel, and if I let this chance go by I feared I would never get to talk with an ice man again.

"Don't you ski?" I asked him, as casually as I could.

He turned his face toward me slowly, as if he'd heard a noise in the distance, and he stared at me with those eyes. Then he calmly shook his head. "I don't ski," he said. "I just like to sit here and read and look at the snow." His words formed white clouds above him, like comic-strip captions. I could actually see the words in the air, until he rubbed them away with a frost-rimed finger.

I had no idea what to say next. I just blushed and stood there. The ice man looked into my eyes and seemed to smile slightly.

"Would you like to sit down?" he asked. "You're interested in me, aren't you? You want to know what an ice man is." Then he laughed. "Relax, there's nothing to worry about. You won't catch a cold just by talking to me."

We sat side by side on a sofa in the corner of the lobby and watched the snowflakes dance outside the window. I ordered a hot cocoa and drank it, but the ice man didn't drink anything. He didn't seem to be any better at conversation than I was. Not only that, but we didn't seem to have anything in common to talk about. At first, we talked about the weather. Then we talked about the hotel. "Are you here by yourself?" I asked the ice man. "Yes," he answered. He asked me if I liked skiing. "Not very much," I said. "I only came because my friends insisted. I actually rarely ski at all."

There were so many things I wanted to know. Was his body really made of ice? What did he eat? Where did he live in the summer? Did he have a family? Things like that. But the ice man didn't talk about himself, and I held back from asking personal questions.

Instead, the ice man talked about me. I know it's hard to believe, but he somehow knew all about me. He knew about the members of my family; he knew my age, my likes and dislikes, the state of my health, the school I was attending, and the friends I was seeing. He even knew things that had happened to me so far in the past that I had long since forgotten them.

"I don't understand," I said, flustered. I felt as if I were naked in front of a stranger. "How do you know so much about me? Can you read people's minds?"

"No, I can't read minds or anything like that. I just know," the ice man said. "I just know. It's as if I were looking deep into ice, and, when I look at you like this, things about you become clearly visible to me."

I asked him, "Can you see my future?"

"I can't see the future," he said slowly. "I can't take any interest in the future at all. More precisely, I have no conception of a future. That's because ice has no future. All it has is the past enclosed within it. Ice is able to preserve things that way—very cleanly and distinctly and as vividly as though they were still alive. That's the essence of ice."

"That's nice," I said and smiled. "I'm relieved to hear that. After all, I don't really want to know what my future is."

WE met again a number of times once we were back in the city. Eventually, we started dating. We didn't go to movies, though, or to coffee shops. We didn't even go to restaurants. The ice man rarely ate anything to speak of. Instead, we always sat on a bench in the park and talked about things—anything except the ice man himself.

"Why is that?" I asked him once. "Why don't you talk about yourself? I want to know more about you. Where were you born? What are your parents like? How did you happen to become an ice man?"

The ice man looked at me for a while, and then he shook his head. "I don't know," he said quietly and clearly, exhaling a puff of white words into the air. "I know the past of everything else. But I myself have no past. I don't know where I was born, or what my parents looked like. I don't even know if I had parents. I have no idea how old I am. I don't know if I have an age at all."

The ice man was as lonely as an iceberg in the dark night.

I FELL seriously in love with this ice man. The ice man loved me just as I was—in the present, without any future. In turn, I loved the ice man just as he was—in the present, without any past. We even started to talk about getting married.

I had just turned twenty, and the ice man was the first person I had really loved. At the time, I couldn't begin to imagine what it meant to love an ice man. But even if I'd fallen in love with a normal man I doubt I'd have had a clearer idea of what love meant.

My mother and my older sister were strongly opposed to my marrying the ice man. "You're too young to get married," they said. "Besides, you don't know a thing about his background. You don't even know where he was born or when. How could we possibly tell our relatives that you're marrying someone like that? Plus, this is an ice man we're talking about, and what are you going to do if he suddenly melts away? You don't seem to understand that marriage requires a real commitment."

Their worries were unfounded, though. After all, an ice man isn't really made of ice. He isn't going to melt, no matter how warm it gets. He's called an ice man because his body is as cold as ice, but what he's made of is different from ice, and it's not the kind of cold that takes away other people's heat.

So we got married. Nobody blessed the wedding, and no friends or relatives were happy for us. We didn't hold a ceremony, and, when it came to having my name entered in his family register, well, the ice man didn't even have one. We just decided, the two of us, that we were married. We bought a little cake and ate it together, and that was our modest wedding.

We rented a tiny apartment, and the ice man made a living by working at a cold-storage meat facility. He could take any amount of cold, and he never felt tired, no matter how hard he worked. So the ice man's employer liked him very much, and paid him a better salary than the other employees. The two of us lived a happy life together, without bothering or being bothered by anyone.

When the ice man made love to me, I saw in my mind a piece of ice that I was sure existed somewhere in quiet solitude. I thought that the ice man probably knew where that piece of ice was. It was frozen hard, so hard that I thought nothing could be harder. It was the biggest piece of ice in the world. It was somewhere very far away, and the ice man was passing on the memories of that ice to me and to the world. At first, I felt confused when the ice man made love to me. But, after a while, I got used to it. I even started to love having sex with the ice man. In the night, we silently shared that enormous piece of ice, in which hundreds of millions of years—all the pasts of the world—were stored.

THERE were no problems to speak of in our married life. We loved each other deeply, and nothing came between us. We wanted to have a child, but that didn't seem to be possible. It may have been that human genes and ice-man genes didn't combine easily. In any case, it was partly because we didn't have children that I found myself with time on my hands. I would finish up all the housework in the morning, and then have nothing to do. I didn't have any friends to talk to or go out with, and I didn't have much to do with the people in our neighborhood, either. My mother and sister were still angry with me for marrying the ice man and showed no sign of ever wanting to see me again. And although, as the months passed, the people around us started talking to him from time to time, deep in their hearts they still hadn't accepted the ice man or me, who had married him. We were different from them, and no amount of time could bridge the gap between us.

So, while the ice man was working, I stayed at home by myself, reading books and listening to music. I tend to prefer staying at home, anyway, and I don't especially mind being alone. But I was still young, and doing the same thing day after day eventually began to bother me. It wasn't the boredom that hurt. It was the repetition.

That was why I said to my husband one day, "How would it be if the two of us went away on a trip somewhere, just for a change?"

"A trip?" the ice man said. He narrowed his eyes and stared at me. "What on earth would we take a trip for? Aren't you happy being here with me?"

"It's not that," I said. "I am happy. But I'm bored. I feel like travelling somewhere far away and seeing things that I've never seen before. I want to see what it's like to breathe new air. Do you understand? Besides, we haven't even had our honeymoon yet. We have some savings, and you have plenty of vacation days coming to you. Isn't it about time that we got away somewhere and took it easy for a while?"

The ice man heaved a deep frozen sigh. It crystallized in midair with a ringing sound. He laced his long fingers together on his knees. "Well, if you really want to go on a trip so badly, I don't have anything against it. I'll go anywhere if it'll make you happy. But do you know where you want to go?"

"How about visiting the South Pole?" I said. I chose the South Pole because I was sure that the ice man would be interested in going somewhere cold. And, to be honest, I had always wanted to travel there. I wanted to wear a fur coat with a hood, and I wanted to see the aurora australis and a flock of penguins.

When I said this, my husband looked straight into my eyes, without blinking, and I felt as if a pointed icicle were piercing all the way through to the back of my head. He was silent for a while, and finally he said, in a glinting voice, "All right, if that's what you want, then let's go to the South Pole. You're really sure that this is what you want?"

I wasn't able to answer right away. The ice man's stare had been on me so long that the inside of my head felt numb. Then I nodded.

AS time passed, though, I came to regret ever having brought up the idea of going to the South Pole. I don't know why, but it seemed that as soon as I spoke the words "South Pole" to my husband something changed inside him. His eyes became sharper, his breath came out whiter, and his fingers were frostier. He hardly talked to me anymore, and he stopped eating entirely. All of this made me feel very insecure.

Five days before we were supposed to leave, I got up my nerve and said, "Let's forget about going to the South Pole. When I think about it now, I realize that it's going to be terribly cold there, and it might not be good for our health. I'm starting to think that it might be better for us to go someplace more ordinary. How about Europe? Let's go have a real vacation in Spain. We can drink wine, eat paella, and see a bullfight or something."

But my husband paid no attention to what I was saying. He stared off into space for a few minutes. Then he declared, "No, I don't particularly want to go to Spain. Spain is too hot for me. It's too dusty, and the food is too spicy. Besides, I've already bought tickets for the South Pole. And we've got a fur coat and fur-lined boots for you. We can't let all that go to waste. Now that we've come this far, we can't not go."

The truth is that I was scared. I had a premonition that if we went to the South Pole something would happen to us that we might not be able to undo. I was having this bad dream over and over again. It was always the same. I'd be out taking a walk and I'd fall into a deep crevasse that had opened up in the ground. Nobody would find me, and I'd freeze down there. Shut up inside the ice, I'd stare up at the sky. I'd be conscious, but I wouldn't be able to move, not even a finger. I'd realize that moment by moment I was becoming the past. As people looked at me, at what I'd become, they were looking at the past. I was a scene moving backward, away from them.

Then I'd wake up and find the ice man sleeping beside me. He always slept without breathing, like a dead man.

But I loved the ice man. I cried, and my tears dripped onto his cheek and he woke up and held me in his arms.

"I had a bad dream," I told him.

"It was only a dream," he said. "Dreams come from the past, not the future. You aren't bound by them. The dreams are bound by you. Do you understand that?"

"Yes," I said, though I wasn't convinced.

I COULDN'T find a good reason to cancel the trip, so in the end my husband and I boarded a plane for the South Pole. The stewardesses were all taciturn. I wanted to look at the view out the window, but the clouds were so thick that I couldn't see anything. After a while, the window was covered with a layer of ice. My husband sat silently reading a book. I felt none of the excitement of heading off on a vacation. I was just going through the motions and doing things that had already been decided on.

When we went down the stairs and stepped off onto the ground of the South Pole, I felt my husband's body lurch. It lasted less than a blink of an eye, just half a second, and his expression didn't change at all, but I saw it happen. Something inside the ice man had been secretly, violently shaken. He stopped and looked at the sky, then at his hands. He heaved a huge breath. Then he looked at me and grinned. He said, "Is this the place you wanted to visit?"

"Yes," I said. "It is."

The South Pole was lonely beyond anything I had expected. Almost no one lived there. There was just one small, featureless town, and in that town there was one hotel, which was, of course, also small and featureless. The South Pole was not a tourist destination. There wasn't a single penguin. And you couldn't see the aurora australis. There were no trees, flowers, rivers, or ponds. Everywhere I went, there was only ice. Everywhere, as far as I could see, the wasteland of ice stretched on and on.

My husband, though, walked enthusiastically from place to place as if he couldn't get enough of it. He learned the local language quickly, and spoke with the townspeople in a voice that had the hard rumble of an avalanche. He conversed with them for hours with a serious expression on his face, but I had no way of knowing what they were talking about. I felt as though my husband had betrayed me and left me to care for myself.

There, in that wordless world surrounded by thick ice, I eventually lost all my strength. Bit by bit, bit by bit. In the end, I didn't even have the energy to feel irritated anymore. It was as though I had lost the compass of my emotions somewhere. I had lost track of where I was heading, I had lost track of time, and I had lost all sense of my own self. I don't know when this started or when it ended, but when I regained consciousness I was in a world of ice, an eternal winter drained of all color, closed in alone.

Even after most of my sensation had gone, I still knew this much. My husband at the South Pole was not the same man as before. He looked out for me just as he had always done, and he spoke to me kindly. I could tell that he truly meant the things he said to me. But I also knew that he was no longer the ice man I had met in the hotel at the ski resort.

There was no way I could bring this to anybody's attention, though. Everyone at the South Pole liked him, and, anyway, they couldn't understand a word I said. Puffing out their white breath, they would tell jokes and argue and sing songs in their own language while I sat by myself in our room, looking out at a gray sky that was unlikely to clear for months to come. The airplane that had brought us there had long since gone, and after a while the runway was covered with a hard layer of ice, just like my heart.

"Winter has come," my husband said. "It's going to be a very long winter, and there will be no more planes, or ships, either. Everything has frozen over. It looks as though we'll have to stay here until next spring."

About three months after we arrived at the South Pole, I realized that I was pregnant. The child that I gave birth to would be a little ice man—I knew this. My womb had frozen over, and my amniotic fluid was slush. I could feel its chill inside me. My child would be just like his father, with eyes like icicles and frost-rimed fingers. And our new family would never again set foot outside the South Pole. The eternal past, heavy beyond all comprehension, had us in its grasp. We would never shake it off.

Now there's almost no heart left in me. My warmth has gone very far away. Sometimes I forget that warmth ever existed. In this place, I am lonelier than anyone else in the world. When I cry, the ice man kisses my cheek, and my tears turn to ice. He takes those frozen teardrops in his hand and puts them on his tongue. "See how I love you," he says. He is telling the truth. But a wind sweeping in from nowhere blows his white words back and back into the past.

—Translated by Richard L. Peterson

VINTAGE BOOKS BY HARUKI MURAKAMI

after the quake

Out of the Kobe earthquake of 1995 come these six surreal (yet somehow believable) stories. An electronics salesman, abruptly deserted by his wife, is entrusted to deliver a mysterious package but gets more than he bargained for on the receiving end; a Thai chauffeur takes his troubled charge to a seer, who penetrates her deepest sorrow; and, in the unforgettable title story, a boy acknowledges a shattering secret about his past that will change his life forever.
Fiction/Literature/0-375-71327-1

Dance Dance Dance

As he searches for a mysteriously vanished girlfriend, Haruki Murakami's protagonist plunges into a wind tunnel of sexual violence and metaphysical dread in which he collides with call girls, plays chaperone to a lovely teenage psychic, and receives cryptic instructions from a shabby but oracular Sheep Man.
Fiction/Literature/0-679-75379-6

The Elephant Vanishes

This collection of stories is a determined assault on the normal. A man sees his favorite elephant vanish into thin

air, a newlywed couple suffers attacks of hunger that drive them to hold up a McDonald's in the middle of the night, and a young woman discovers that she has become irresistible to a little green monster in her back yard.
Fiction/Literature/0-679-75053-3

Hard-Boiled Wonderland and the End of the World

Murakami draws readers into a narrative particle accelerator in which a split-brained data processor, a deranged scientist, his shockingly undemure granddaughter, Bob Dylan, and various thugs, librarians, and subterranean monsters collide to dazzling effect.
Fiction/Literature/0-679-74346-4

Norwegian Wood

Toru, a college student in Tokyo, is devoted to Naoko, a beautiful and introspective young woman. But their relationship is colored by the tragic death of their mutual best friend years before. Toru has learned to live with his grief, but it becomes apparent that for Naoko, life is becoming too difficult to bear. As she retreats further into her own world, Toru finds himself reaching out to others and drawn to a fiercely independent and sexually liberated young woman.
Fiction/Literature/0-375-70402-7

South of the Border, West of the Sun

Born in 1951 to an affluent family, Hajime has arrived at middle age wanting for almost nothing. The postwar years have brought him a fine marriage, two daughters, and an enviable career. Yet a nagging sense of inauthenticity about his success threatens Hajime's happiness. A boyhood memory of a wise, lonely girl named Shimamoto clouds his heart.

Fiction/Literature/0-679-76739-8

Sputnik Sweetheart

Plunging us into an urbane Japan of jazz bars, coffee shops, Jack Kerouac, and the Beatles, Murakami tells a story of a tangled triangle of uniquely unrequited loves. A college student, "K," falls in love with his classmate, Sumire. When Sumire disappears from an island off the coast of Greece, "K" is solicited to join the search party and finds himself drawn back into her world, and beset by ominous, haunting visions.

Fiction/Literature/0-375-72605-5

Underground

On March 20, 1995, five members of the religious cult Aum Shinrikyo conducted chemical warfare on the Tokyo subway system using sarin, a poison gas twenty-six times as

deadly as cyanide. In an attempt to discover why, Murakami talked to the people who lived through the catastrophe—from a Subway Authority employee with survivor guilt, to a fashion salesman with more venom for the media than for the perpetrators, to a young cult member who vehemently condemns the attack though he has not quit Aum.
Nonfiction/Literature/0-375-72580-6

A Wild Sheep Chase

A marvelous hybrid of mythology and mystery, *A Wild Sheep Chase* is the extraordinary literary thriller that launched Haruki Murakami's international reputation. A young advertising exec uses a postcard picture of a sheep in a campaign, unwittingly capturing the attention of a man in black who offers a menacing ultimatum: find the sheep or face dire consequences.
Fiction/Literature/0-375-71894-X

The Wind-Up Bird Chronicle

The Wind-Up Bird Chronicle is at once a detective story, an account of a disintegrated marriage, and an excavation of the buried secrets of World War II. In a Tokyo suburb a young man named Toru Okada searches for his wife's missing cat. Soon he finds himself looking for his wife as well in a netherworld that lies beneath the placid surface of Tokyo.
Fiction/Literature/0-679-77543-9

VINTAGE READERS

Authors available in this series

Martin Amis
James Baldwin
Sandra Cisneros
Joan Didion
Richard Ford
Langston Hughes
Barry Lopez
Alice Munro
Haruki Murakami
Vladimir Nabokov
V. S. Naipaul
Oliver Sacks

Representing a wide spectrum of some of our most significant modern authors, the Vintage Readers offer an attractive, accessible selection of writing that matters.